5
SUGAR CREEK GANG
The CHICAGO ADVENTURE

Paul Hutchens

MOODY PRESS
CHICAGO

PREFACE

Hi—from a member of the Sugar Creek Gang!

It's just that I don't know which one I am. When I was good, I was Little Jim. When I did bad things—well, sometimes I was Bill Collins or even mischievous Poetry.

You see, I am the daughter of Paul Hutchens, and I spent many an hour listening to him read his manuscript as far as he had written it that particular day. I went along to the north woods of Minnesota, to Colorado, and to the various other places he would go to find something different for the Gang to do.

Now the years have passed—more than fifty, actually. My father is in heaven, but the Gang goes on. All thirty-six books are still in print and now are being updated for today's readers with input from my five children, who also span the decades from the '50s to the '70s.

The real Sugar Creek is in Indiana, and my father and his six brothers were the original Gang. But the idea of the books and their ministry were and are the Lord's. It is He who keeps the Gang going.

PAULINE HUTCHENS WILSON

1

Roaring along through the sky 5,000 feet high—which is almost a mile—and at 400 miles an hour was the most thrilling experience of my life up to that time.

Well, come to think of it, I guess riding on the waves of a mad lake, with nothing to hold me up except a life-preserver vest, was really the most thrilling as well as the craziest. As I told you in my last story about the Sugar Creek Gang, being tossed around by those big angry waves was like being scared half to death riding on a Tilt-A-Whirl at a county fair.

I had thought maybe an airplane ride would be even worse. It wasn't at all, but, boy, oh boy, was it different!

Of course none of us thought that Dragonfly, who is the balloon-eyed member of our gang, would get a bad case of vertigo and have to have the stewardess give him first aid to bring him back to normal again. In fact, the pilot actually had to come down to a lower altitude before Dragonfly was all right.

That's getting too far ahead of the story though, and I'll have to wait a chapter or two before I explain what vertigo means.

I'm going to be a doctor when I grow up, you know, and that's why I'm learning the names of all the medical terms I can while I'm little, which I'm not actually anymore. I'm already ten and three-fourths years old and have red hair and—but it wouldn't be fair to tell you about myself before introducing the rest of the gang.

The Sugar Creek Gang is the most important gang in the whole country, maybe. Anyway, we have more twisted-up adventures than most anybody else in the world, and so far they have all come out all right.

Maybe I'd better take time right now to introduce the members of the gang to you—and to explain why we were taking an airplane ride and where to.

You remember that Circus, who is our acrobat and who also has an acrobatic voice that can climb the musical scale even better than he can climb a tree, had been invited to a big Chicago church to sing over the radio on Thanksgiving Day. Well, the date was changed, and he was going to sing at what is called a youth rally on Labor Day weekend in September instead, and all the gang was going with him.

Little Jim, the littlest and the grandest guy in the gang, and maybe in the whole world, had to go with him to accompany him on the piano anyway, he being an expert pianist. So, of course, we all wanted to go along, and our parents had said we could—that is, they had *finally* said we could.

It took my brownish-gray-haired mom quite a while to make up her mind to let me go, and I had to wash dishes every noon for all the rest of

the summer ju...
even had to do th...
didn't, although I wa...
enough not to say so.

The day Mom finally
was one of the hottest days w...
actually never had felt such *tire...
my life. You could lie right down
a dinner of fried chicken, noodles, ...d
mashed potatoes, and raspberry shortca... and
go to sleep in less than a minute. You could stay
asleep all the way through dishwashing time—
that is, if Mom didn't get tired of waiting for
you to come and help, and call you.

You could even sleep better if you knew
that, after the dishes were done, there were
potatoes to hoe and beans to pick. But if you
happened to be going swimming, or if there
was going to be a gang meeting, you weren't
even sleepy.

That afternoon there were beans to be
picked, so as soon as I had finished my shortcake, I asked to be excused. Dad said yes and
let me get up and go into our living room,
which was the coolest room in the house, and
lie down on the floor until Mom had the dishes
ready.

Mom's floor was always clean, but even at
that she always made me lay a paper on it before I could put a pillow down to sleep on. I
hadn't any more than lain down, it seemed,
when her voice came sizzling in from the kitchen
and woke me up.

...ake up any more than I did ...e. I'd been dreaming the craziest ... Anyway, it seemed crazy at the time, and anybody would have laughed at it. I never realized, while I was dreaming, that something was going to happen almost like that in real life after we got to Chicago.

I dreamed that I was already a doctor and that I was in a hospital with a lot of nurses in white all around. Also, all around and overhead, airplane engines were droning. One of the members of the Sugar Creek Gang had eaten too much raspberry shortcake and had a stomachache, and the only thing that would help him was for me, the doctor, to give him a blood transfusion. In my dream I was pouring raspberry juice into one of the veins of his arm through a little tin funnel, and he was crying and saying, "I don't like to wash dishes! I don't want to!"

That was when Mom called me to wake up and come to help her.

I woke up halfway at first, and I was as cross as anything, which any doctor will tell you is natural for anybody when he gets waked up without wanting to be.

But my dad, who is a Christian and knows the Bible from A to Z—and not only says he is a Christian, but actually acts like one at home as well as in church—he says the Bible says, "Be angry, and yet do not sin." And that means if somebody or something makes you angry, you ought to tie up your anger, the way people do a mad bull, and not let it run wild.

Dad says a boy's temper under control is like a fire in a stove, useful for many things. But when it isn't controlled, it's like a fire in a hay-mow or a forest. Some people actually die many years sooner than they ought to because they get mad so many times and stay mad so long it makes them sick.

Maybe my dad tells me these things especially because I'm red-haired and maybe am too quick-tempered. He says if I don't lose my temper all the time, but keep it under control, it'll help me do many important things while I'm growing up.

So, as angry as I was for being waked up and for having to do dishes, I tied up my anger as quick as I could. I didn't say a word or grumble or anything. I didn't even frown.

By the way, do you know how many muscles of your face have to work to make a fierce-looking frown? Maybe you wouldn't believe it, but it actually takes sixty-five, our teacher says. And it takes only thirteen muscles to make a smile. So it's a waste of energy to go around frowning when you're already tired and lazy.

While on the way from the living room to the kitchen to help Mom, I remembered something Dad had told me one day when I was going around our barnyard with a big scowl on my very freckled face. This is what he said: "Bill Collins, you're making the same face while you're a boy that you'll have to look at in the mirror all the rest of your life."

That had made me scowl deeper than ever, and I went toward the barn still scowling but not saying anything. The minute I got into the barn, though, I took out of my pocket a little round mirror that I was carrying and looked at myself. And because I was angry, I scowled and scowled and made a fierce face and stuck out my tongue at myself and hated myself for a while.

Then I saw a big, long brown rat dart across the barn floor, and in a flash I was chasing after it and calling old Mixy-cat to come and do her work and see to it that there weren't so many live rats around the Collins family's barn.

What Dad had said didn't soak in at all until one day Mom told me almost the same thing, only in different words.

My mom has the kindest face I ever saw, and her forehead is very smooth, without any deep creases in it—either going across it or running up and down. Just for fun one day I asked her if she'd been ironing it, it was so smooth, and do you know what she said?

She said, "I've been ironing it all my life. I've kept the frowns and wrinkles off ever since I was a little girl, so the muscles that make frowns and wrinkles won't have a chance to grow"—which they will if they get too much exercise.

So it would be better for even a girl to be cheerful while she's little enough to be still growing, so she'll have a face like my mom's when she gets big.

Well, I thought all those thoughts even before I was halfway to the kitchen. On the way, I stepped into our downstairs bedroom for a half jiffy to look at Charlotte Ann. She was my one-year-old baby sister and had pretty brownish-red curls and several small freckles on her nose. She was supposed to be sleeping and wasn't. She was lying there holding a toy in one hand and shaking it and trying to take it apart to see what made it rattle.

I stood looking down at her pretty pink cheeks, and her brownish-red hair, and her chubby little fists, and at the kind of disgusted pucker on her forehead because the toy wouldn't come apart.

"Listen, Charlotte Ann," I said, scowling at her, "you're making the same kind of face now you'll have to look at in the mirror all the rest of your life. You've got to think pretty thoughts if you want to have a pretty face."

Then I went out into the kitchen and washed my hands with soap, which is what you're supposed to do before you dry dishes, or else maybe Mom will have to wash the dishes over again and the drying towel too.

I still felt cranky, but I kept thinking about the airplane trip the gang was going to take to Chicago—all the gang except me, so far—so I kept my fire in the stove. I knew that pretty soon my parents would have to decide something, and I kept on hoping it would be "Yes."

My mom had been teaching me to sing tenor, and sometimes on Sunday nights, when she'd play the organ in our front room, she and Dad and I would sing trios, which helped to make us all like each other better. So while we were doing dishes that noon, Mom and I started singing different songs we used in school and also some of the gospel songs we used in church. And the next thing we knew, the dishes were done and put away, and I was free to go and pick beans if I wanted to, or if I didn't want to.

I was wishing I could run lickety-sizzle out across our yard, through the gate, across the dusty gravel road, and vault over the rail fence on the other side. I'd fly down the path through the woods, down the hill past the big birch tree to the spring, where the gang was supposed to meet at two o'clock, if they could. Sometimes we couldn't because most of us had to work some of the time. Today was one of the days I couldn't.

As soon as I'd finished the last dish, which was our big long platter that had had the fried chicken on it, I went back into our bathroom. I looked past my ordinary-looking face and saw my dad's reflection in the mirror. He was standing outside our bathroom window, which was closed tight to keep out some of the terrific heat that was outdoors. Standing right beside him was Old Man Paddler.

For those of you who've never heard of Old Man Paddler, I'd better say that he's one of the best friends the Sugar Creek Gang ever had or ever will have. He lives up in the hills above Sugar Creek and likes kids, and he has put us boys into his will, which he says he's already made.

He and my dad were standing there talking, and the old man's gnarled hands were gesturing around in a sort of circle, and he was moving them up and down and pointing toward the sky.

Right away I guessed he was talking about the airplane trip to Chicago. I could see his long white whiskers bobbing up and down the way a man's whiskers do when he's talking. All of a sudden, he and Dad reached out and shook hands and then started walking toward the porch.

All of another sudden a great thrill came running and jumped *kersmack* into the middle of my heart. I was so happy it began to hurt inside terribly, because somehow I knew that I was going to get to go with the rest of the gang.

And just that minute, as Dad was opening the screen door to our kitchen to let Old Man Paddler in first, Dad said, "All right, we'll let him go!"

My hands weren't even dry when I left that bathroom. In fact, I hardly saw the towel that slipped from the rack where I'd tossed it up in too big a hurry. I wanted to make a dive for that old man's whiskers and hug him. Instead, I just stood there trembling and seeing myself sailing along through the air with big white clouds all around our airplane and the earth away down below.

Pretty soon we were all in the living room, where it was cooler than in the kitchen, and were all sitting on different chairs. I had my bare feet twisted around and underneath my chair and fastened onto the rounds and was rocking back and forth, noticing that with every rock the chair crept sideways a little over the rug.

It was kind of like a meeting of some sort at first, with all of us sitting quiet. Then Dad cleared his throat and said in his big voice, "Well, Bill, Mr. Paddler has persuaded us to let him invest a little money in you. He wants to pay your way to Chicago by airplane. His nephew, Barry Boyland, has agreed to come and be chaperone to the whole Sugar Creek Gang."

There was a twinkle in the old man's eyes, several of them in Dad's, and also some in Mom's. Dad finished by saying that the beans could be picked later in the day when it was cooler, and that I really ought to meet with the gang today, if I wanted to, and—

As quick as I could, after I'd courteously thanked the kind, trembling-voiced old man, I was out of the house, running through the heat waves, toward our front gate. I frisked across the road, stirring up a lot of dust, and vaulted over the rail fence. Then I went like greased lightning toward the spring, imagining myself to be an airplane and trying to make a noise like one, wishing I *was* one, and almost bursting to tell the news to the rest of the gang.

My dad's last words were ringing in my ears as I flew through the woods, with my voice droning like an airplane. This is what he said while we were still in the living room: "Of course, Bill, we shall expect you to keep your eyes open and learn a lot of things while you're there. Make it an educational trip as well as a pleasure trip."

My own answer was very quick. "Sure," I said, already halfway across the room to the door.

I remembered my promise later, though— and kept it too, when I wrote a letter to my parents from Chicago.

Zzzzz-rrrrrr! On my way to the spring!

2

The minute I got to the top of the hill that is just above the spring where our gang nearly always meets, I looked down and saw nearly all the gang there, sprawled on the long, mashed-down green-and-brown grass, each one lying in a different direction. As usual, Circus was perched on a limb of a tree, chattering like a monkey, getting ready to do an acrobatic stunt of some kind.

I dashed past the old beech tree that has all our initials carved on its smooth gray bark and, after turning a somersault, was soon lying down beside everybody, panting and trying to stop breathing so hard. I tell you, it felt good to know I had good news for them, and it felt good to be with the gang again, after thinking all day that I'd have to pick beans instead of being allowed to go in swimming.

Good old gang! I thought, still panting.

There was Poetry, the barrel-shaped member of the gang, who has maybe the keenest mind of all of us, especially when it comes to arithmetic. We named him Poetry because he knows so many different poems, and any minute something might remind him of one. Then we'd either have to listen to it or else shush him up, if we could. He was my best friend most of the time. He and Circus were always in a good-natured argument with each other.

In fact, they were in one that very minute. Circus called down from the limb of the tree where he was and said, "Say, Poetry, do you know why I like you?"

"Why?" Poetry's squawky voice called up to him.

"'Cause," Circus called back down, "'cause in the winter I can use you for a windbreak to keep the cold wind off, and in the summertime I can lie down behind you in the shade to keep cool."

It was a very old joke, but we laughed anyway.

Circus came sliding down out of his tree right that minute to lie down beside Poetry on the shady side of him, which started a good-natured fight.

I told the gang my good news. Then I told them the crazy dream I'd had about the doctor, who was myself, giving a blood transfusion with raspberry juice.

That reminded Big Jim that one time, before he'd moved into Sugar Creek territory, he'd had to have a blood transfusion himself, because he had been hurt in a mowing machine accident. He rolled up his right trouser leg to show us a white scar with a lot of stitch scars from one end of it to the other, making it look like a long white worm with eight pairs of legs. We'd seen the scar before, but I just never told you about it.

Then Big Jim rolled over and sat up and grinned and said, "I have a special kind of blood, which is called type B. Not more than seven people in a hundred have it. They had a hard time finding anybody to give me his blood, and I almost died."

Of course, I was interested in that, since I was going to be a doctor. We all let him tell his story over again, even though we'd heard it a good many times.

Then we talked about what we'd like to see when we got to Chicago. Little Jim said he wanted to visit the zoo to see if maybe his pet bear was there. He'd had one once and had to sell it to some zoo when it got too big and too cross to be a pet.

When he mentioned the bear, I looked over at him, and there were tears in his eyes. He'd really liked that cub very much.

That brave little guy had saved all our lives once. He'd shot the cub's fierce mother when she was so mad she could have killed all of us.

But I'd better not get started on that story. *This* story is about the Sugar Creek Gang in Chicago, so I can't get off on that exciting bear's tale now.

Also, Little Jim said, he wanted to go to one of the big department stores when we got to Chicago and ride up and down on an escalator.

Big Jim wanted to see the Federal Reserve Bank, because he's interested in business and wants to be a banker sometime. Big Jim is the oldest member of our gang. He has fuzz on his upper lip most of the time, was once a Boy Scout, and has the best manners. He is always especially courteous to Sylvia, our minister's oldest daughter, and can lick the stuffing out of any boy his age.

Big Jim still has a scar on the knuckles of his right hand where the skin was split open on a bank robber's jaw once. *That* was some experience! The Sugar Creek Gang captured that robber in the middle of the night, saving Old Man Paddler's life. And if we hadn't, we wouldn't be having our free airplane trip to Chicago!

That's another thing I found out. The old man was going to pay *all* our fares himself and also pay his nephew, Barry Boyland, a salary while he was being our chaperone. Barry, you know, was the big, brown-faced, grand young man who took us on our camping trip up north.

Well, there we were, lying in the grass just above the spring, talking, laughing, doing stunts, each one trying to say something funnier than the other one. Big Jim, Little Jim, Circus, Dragonfly, Poetry, and—oh, yes—Tom Till.

Little Tom is the new member of our gang and has red hair and can't help it. For a minute, while we were lying there, I looked over at his nose and noticed that it was nice and straight where I'd once smashed it in a fight, and it looked like any boy's nose ought to.

Tom's parents were poor, mostly because his dad spent most of his money for whiskey.

Tom's dad is always bragging about how he can take a drink of whiskey or else leave it alone, whichever he wants to. Dad says every sad old man in the world who is a drunk now used to brag about how he could take a drink or else leave it alone when he wanted to.

Maybe I'd better say too that Tom's big brother Bob had been licked good and hard once in a fight with Big Jim, and that he hated Big Jim terribly and might do most anything to get even with him.

And while I'm telling you about drinking people, I ought to tell you that Circus's dad used to be one, but he's what the Bible calls "born again" now, and his money goes into clothes and food and shoes for his family instead of into his stomach, which is getting well again after having ulcers.

And that's all the Sugar Creek Gang except me, Bill Collins, whose real and full name is William Jasper Collins, a name I don't like and which my parents call me sometimes when I haven't been behaving myself. I'd actually rather be good than to have them call me that.

We were lying there, each of us chewing on the end of different pieces of grass, as boys do. For a minute I thought of how cows sometimes lie down like that and chew the grass they've already eaten, swallowing backward to bring it up into their mouths. Then, when they've chewed it all they want to, they swallow it down into their other stomach and manufacture it into milk. Just as I was thinking of how our little Charlotte Ann was getting big enough to stop drinking milk out of a bottle and to drink it like a human being, I heard a noise up the creek.

It sounded like a lot of boys swimming in *our* swimming hole!

Big Jim jerked his head up real quick, making me think not of a cow but of a general in an army.

If there was anything our gang didn't like, it was for an outside gang of boys to come into Sugar Creek territory and act as if they owned the place. That's why we'd had the fierce Battle of Bumblebee Hill the summer before, when Big Bob Till and his gang of rough town boys had come out and eaten up our strawberries. That was the time Big Jim had licked Big Bob for the first time Bob had ever been licked, and also the time when I'd smashed little red-haired Tom's nose, and all the rest of us had licked all the rest of *them*.

So, while I was lying there, sprawled out like a small cow, listening to the hollering up the creek, my fists began to double up, and my temper started to get hot. I could see the rest of the gang was feeling the same way. There really wasn't anything very selfish about our gang, and we wouldn't have cared much if other people used our swimming hole, if they'd *ask* and be careful not to spoil it. But the last time Bob's gang had been there, they'd broken down the two or three pretty little ash saplings on which we usually hung our clothes, and they'd turned our diving raft upside down and left it with mud smeared all over the top.

I rolled over, bumping into Poetry and getting stopped as though I had bumped into a stone wall, at the very moment Dragonfly, who is always seeing things first, said, "Look! There's our raft floating downstream!"

And sure enough it was—upside down and floating right toward where we were. In fact it looked as if it would bump into the bank right in front of the spring.

Well, that was too much. It looked like there was going to be another famous battle.

We scrambled to our feet. That is, we started to, but Big Jim stopped us by saying, "Ssh! Lie down. *All* of you. Keep still! Wait till I see what the note says."

What note? I thought. Then I saw a piece of paper lying on top of the raft, and a big rock lying on top of it to hold it down, so the wind wouldn't blow it off.

As the rest of us kept still and lay where we were, Big Jim stood up with a grim face and walked over to the spring and down the steep little bank to the edge of the creek. He *made* us lie still, or we wouldn't have, because that raft upside down was like a red flag being waved in front of seven mad bulls that weren't tied.

I looked over the top of Poetry to Little Jim, and he was holding onto his stick, which he nearly always carried, very tight, so tight that his knuckles were white.

In a flash, Big Jim had his clothes off and

was wading and swimming out toward the raft. In another flash, he was dragging the raft after him toward our shore, while we lay like the springs in a bunch of jack-in-the-boxes, waiting for somebody to press the button.

"See!" Dragonfly hissed. "See where they cut the ropes! Our *new ropes!*"

I was already seeing it. They'd cut the lines that we'd put on the raft to anchor it to the bottom.

Big Jim used one of the ropes to tie the raft to the root of a tree that grew there on the bank of the creek. Then he lifted the rock off the piece of paper, and without even stopping to dress, because he wasn't dry yet anyway, he picked up his clothes and came back to where we were.

I could see the big muscles on his arms, especially the ones between his shoulders and his elbows, which are called the biceps muscles, and I thought how much bigger they were than mine and also how hard they were when he tensed them. Our gang was always showing each other our biceps and looking proud because each week they seemed a little bigger and harder, but weren't.

Well, Big Jim handed the note to Poetry, who sat up and read it, his squawky voice sounding more than ever like a duck with a bad cold and also as if he was having a chill. His hand was shaking a little too, while he held it, and this is what he read:

To the Sugar Creek Gang:

Gentlemen and cowards! A swimming hole is no place for a choir platform. Anyway, we can't use it, so we're shipping it down to you, express collect. If you don't like it, you can lump it!

Well, the minute Poetry finished reading the note out loud, we were all ready to fight. It was an insult. Maybe you know that the Sugar Creek Gang all went to church every Sunday and weren't ashamed of it. In fact, anybody in the world that wants to amount to a hill of soup beans ought to go to church.

"It's an *insult!*" Poetry squawked. "Let's go up there and lick the stuffin's out of them!"

By that time we were all rolled over on our stomachs and were waiting for orders from Big Jim.

"Read the signature," Poetry said and passed the note to Big Jim.

Big Jim looked at it, and we all squirmed around and read over his shoulders, and this is what it said:

Yours truly,
THE HELLFIRE GANG

The silly bunch of copycats! I thought. My dad had told me once that more than a hundred years ago, when a famous evangelist was preaching in a town, there was a wild gang of boys there who had called themselves The Hellfire Club.

Anyway, maybe you know that Bob Till's dad didn't believe in God and that Bob and little red-haired Tom had never been to Sunday school in their lives until I had got Tom to start going with the Collins family.

The next thing I knew, Big Jim had folded the paper and tucked it into one of the pockets of his overalls, which right that minute he was starting to pull on. He did it very slowly, as if he was thinking. His jaw was set hard, and his lips were pressed together in a straight line, which meant plenty.

But when he got through dressing, he plunked himself down on the grass again! With fists still doubled up, he stared out across the woods toward a stump, where I saw a little reddish-brown chipmunk sitting straight up, holding an acorn or something in its forepaws and eating very, very fast, the way chipmunks do. Then Big Jim rolled over and lay in the sun.

What? I thought. *Are we going to lie here like a bunch of saps and let the Hellfire Gang spoil our swimming hole?*

Then I looked over the top of Dragonfly's head and saw Little Tom Till's messed-up red hair and his five or six hundred freckles and his bright blue eyes, which looked kind of like there was a sad fire in them. And I knew there wasn't going to be any fight, and why. Big Jim simply wouldn't lead the gang into battle under such circumstances.

It's a terrible letdown, though, to be all keyed up for a good fight and then not get to have it, especially when you know the other gang needs a licking. I remembered our other fight, when Big Jim had led us to victory. I remembered the way he did it. How he stepped out from the bushes where he had been lying in ambush. How he walked stiff-legged, the way a dog does when it walks out toward a new dog it's never seen before. How he looked up to the top of the hill, where Bob and his gang stood calling us all kinds of names. How Big Jim stood there and said, "Fellows, it isn't a question of whether we're afraid to fight. There isn't a man among us that's got a drop of coward's blood in him!"

We still didn't have any of that kind of blood, but we didn't dare fight with Little Tom belonging to *our* gang and his brother belonging to the other. It wouldn't be fair to Tom.

I had to tell you about this almost-fight, though, so you'll understand what happened in Chicago when Big Jim and Bob met again under the strangest circumstances you ever saw.

Of course, none of us knew that Bob would be in Chicago ahead of us. And certainly none of us ever dreamed why he'd be there, but he was.

3

It was the morning before we were to leave for Chicago that I found out Bob Till had gone there ahead of us.

Mom and Dad and I were sitting at the breakfast table, each one of us having finished eating. Charlotte Ann was in her crib in the other room. Dad reached over to a corner of the table for our Bible, which was always on that corner at mealtime.

All of us knew that we would have what we called "family devotions" at our house at least once a day, and we usually had it at the table. Sometimes Dad would read, sometimes Mom, and sometimes me. Once in a while, we just passed around what is called a "Bread Box," which is a little square box full of Bible verses printed on cards.

Dad picked up the Bible, and I sat quiet, ready to listen. Even though I was anxious to get outdoors and feel the ground under my bare feet—and even though Jenny Wren was outside on our clothesline just whooping it up with a song that sounded like a lot of beautiful gibberish all mixed up with different tones—I knew the Bible was the most important book in the world and that I was supposed to listen politely. Little Jim's mom had taught him, and he had told me, that it was full of "sweet music."

Well, Dad opened the Bible respectfully and asked me to read, which I had started to do when there was a knock on our screen door.

We were eating breakfast in our kitchen, so the door wasn't very far behind me. I turned around and looked, and there, sort of half sitting and half standing on the steps, was Tom Till, the only Christian in the whole Till family, looking very sad, as though something had happened to him.

"Come in, Tom," Mom said, going to the screen door and opening it.

Little Tom bashfully came in and looked around at the different things in the kitchen, such as our new refrigerator and gas stove, which we used especially in the summer instead of our wood stove so Mom wouldn't half smother to death getting meals for the Collins family.

"We're having family devotions," I said.

Dad reached behind him for a chair, and Tom sat down between him and me. Just that minute Charlotte Ann started a funny cooing noise in the other room, but she wasn't crying, so Mom didn't go to get her. Charlotte Ann always half sang and half gurgled in the morning when she was feeling good, which she nearly always was.

I knew Tom Till didn't know what family devotions were, which most boys in the world don't because their parents are not like mine and maybe don't know God well enough to talk to Him.

Pretty soon I was reading the passage Dad had picked out, and it was about people giving their bodies to God so He could use them to do what needed to be done in the world. Just like a great musician playing on a violin or a piano, so we were supposed to let God play on us or else use us like a carpenter uses his tools to build something.

Tom Till's red hair and my red hair were so close together and only a little different in color that for a minute I let my mind stray to the pretty two-tone car that Dad had bought just the other day.

Mom had a notebook in her hand, and she wrote down one of the best verses I'd read. She did that at every family devotions meeting we had, and then, once every week or whenever we wanted to, we checked back over the verses we'd talked about and recalled the different things they meant.

Dad explained to Tom why we did that. "A boy who goes to Sunday school every Sunday for a year still only gets about twenty-six hours a year of Bible instruction, and that isn't very much out of eight thousand seven hundred sixty hours in a year."

It didn't take us long, but when we got through, I understood what the verses meant. If God had my whole body, including my mind, hands, feet, eyes, ears, and all of me, I'd be a great guy, which I really wasn't most of the time.

If He had my eyes, I wouldn't look at things I oughtn't to. If He had my feet, I wouldn't let them carry me places I oughtn't go. If He had my ears, I wouldn't listen to the tough boys' filthy talk at school. And if He had my tongue, I'd tell them in no uncertain terms that their words sounded like the mud in our barnyard looked. And I wouldn't fuss or whine when my parents told me to do something my lazy body didn't want to do. And I'd be polite and wouldn't talk back to them, even when I thought maybe they might have made a mistake in something they accused me of doing and I hadn't done it.

I never saw anybody look so interested—and also as though he was all stirred up inside—as Tom Till. When we'd finished saying things about the verses I'd read, and Mom had finished writing down one of them especially, Dad started to sing the chorus of a church hymn, and I joined in with a kind of tenor and Mom with an alto.

Tom didn't know the song at all and didn't have much of a voice for singing anyway, so he just listened.

We finished the chorus, and Dad got ready to pray. "Are there any requests?" he asked, as he nearly always does.

"Pray for Old Man Paddler," I said. "He doesn't feel very well."

"Pray for our minister," Mom said, and I thought right away of Sylvia, our new minister's oldest daughter, whom Big Jim seemed to like better than anybody.

Then my mind flashed to Circus's sort of ordinary-looking sister, who wasn't saved yet, whom I'd tried to kill a spider for last year at school and didn't because of her thinking I was afraid of it and killing it herself. And even though I didn't much like girls and I especially didn't like her, I thought she ought to be saved anyway.

So I said, "Pray for—" And then I felt the roots of my hair acting as if they were worms and were all starting to crawl at once. I knew that if I had been looking at my freckled face in the mirror, I'd be blushing.

Dad looked at me, and I bowed my head and shut my eyes and shut up, and he said to Tom, "Any requests? Anything or anybody *you* want us to pray for?"

I'd forgotten Tom for a minute, so I opened my eyes again, and I saw him swallow as though he'd forgotten to chew a big bite of something.

Then he said, "Pray for B-Bob. He's—he ran away this morning—"

Dad prayed only a very few minutes, and in language we could all understand. Then at the end of his prayer, he prayed for all our gang by name and especially for Big Bob Till, who it seemed he already knew about.

I thought it was sort of funny that he prayed for Mr. Simondson, our grocer, right along with Bob, and it wasn't until afterward that I found out that Bob Till had broken into his store last night and stolen money out of the cash register.

After breakfast, when Tom and I were outdoors getting ready to dig potatoes, which he had come over to our house to help me do that day—my mom having hired him on purpose so he would have a little spending money when he got to Chicago—I asked him where Bob had gone.

"I don't know," he said, poking one of his bare toes into the soft dirt of our garden. "Maybe he went to Chicago. He's been a-wantin' to go there for a long time."

"Chicago?" I said.

And he said, "Ssh! Not so loud. And please don't tell anybody, or the police'll get him."

I felt sorry for Tom, and I knew if he'd had parents like mine or like the parents most of the boys in our gang had, Bob would have been different and would have had Bible verses growing in his heart and mind instead of a lot of big nasty sins like the tall ugly weeds that grew on both sides of the path on the way to our potato patch.

There wouldn't have been any big weeds there, I thought, if I'd pulled them up or cut them down when they were little.

Anyway, I got to wondering what if we found Bob Till somewhere when we got to Chicago, and I wished we would. In fact, I kind of *knew* we would.

Tom and I worked hard digging potatoes until ten o'clock, when Mom called us to come in and have a cup of chocolate milk. My mom did it more for Tom's sake than for mine. I have enough vitamins in my diet, but Tom's eyes always looked as if he needed more food of some kind.

We dropped our potato forks and walked back to the house. When we got to the lawn, we started stepping on the gray dandelion heads, doing it all the way to the back door, looking like football players trying to dodge somebody on the other team. I was always doing that in our kitchen too—walking around and stepping on my favorite patterns on the linoleum, until Mom's nerves couldn't stand it any longer, and then I'd go outdoors a while.

I didn't even tell Mom or Dad what Tom had told me about Bob. That day finally passed by, with the thing in my mind almost all the time: *Big Bob Till is in Chicago. Big Bob Till is in Chicago, where the Sugar Creek Gang is going.*

At last the next day came. I was up early and acting almost like a chicken with its head cut off.

Dad and Poetry's dad drove us all to the nearest big city where there was an airport. We drove right down through the center of town, and it seemed as if everybody turned to look at us—or else at Dad's new two-tone car.

Old Man Paddler was sitting in the front seat with him. "I wish I were young enough to learn to drive," the old man said, his whiskers bobbing.

Pretty soon we were at the airport and inside the terminal, where Barry Boyland, the old man's nephew, was getting our tickets and where our baggage was being checked for weight, each one of us being allowed to take not more than forty pounds of luggage. Our tickets had been ordered ahead of time, or else we couldn't have gone, because these days more and more people are traveling by air and you have to have reservations.

This was my first visit to an airport terminal. It was almost like a train station, with chairs all around the wall. There was a soda fountain on one end and a place to buy your favorite kind of pop.

On the other side of the ticket window was a control room where two men had earphones on their heads, listening and talking the way people do who are technicians in a little airport.

All of us sat beside each other in a long row, with Little Jim on one side of me and Poetry on the other. I'd been reading up on airplanes almost all summer—at least after we knew we were going to ride in one—so I explained nearly everything to Little Jim, while we were waiting for our plane to come.

"What are those men doing over there?" he asked, motioning toward the technicians.

"They're probably talking to the pilots up in some airplane," I said, and Big Jim finished explaining by saying, "They're using a radio telephone to tell them about weather conditions."

Weather conditions, you know, are very important for airplane officers to know about. I was glad it was a sunny day with only scattered clouds, although I knew a day could start like that at Sugar Creek and before afternoon came there could be a terrific thunderstorm. I hoped there wouldn't be one while we were up there in the middle of where storms come from.

I couldn't any more stay seated than anything, and neither could the rest of us. As soon as they would let us, we went outside and stood just outside the heavy woven-wire fence to watch the baggage and mail trucks moving around and to look at the different people and to wait.

Away off to the right was a hangar where a lot of little airplanes were going up and coming down all the time, maybe taking up passengers or else maybe teaching young pilots.

All of a sudden there was a mighty roaring in the sky, and then we saw our plane circling, getting ready to come down. I was tingling inside, half scared to death. I thought it looked like a long, roundish house with a lot of windows and two wings spread out like an eagle's. It looked fierce as it came taxiing along the runway straight toward the terminal, bigger and bigger, longer and longer, with the propellers of its engines whirling around like two big windmills. It stopped right in front of us.

Somebody pushed a little stairway on wheels up to the plane, a door opened in the side, and some smiling, important-looking people came down the portable stairway. The plane had a few minutes to stay, so people could get off and stretch and look around if they wanted to.

Somebody pushed a hand truck up to the

mail and baggage compartments in the plane's long nose, just between its two eyes, which were the propellers and which weren't turning now.

Poetry and I were standing right beside the gate, watching the people coming off the plane, and the pilot and the copilot and the stewardess, who was smiling and wearing dark glasses and light shoes and a brownish suit like one Little Jim's mom wears sometimes. The stewardess and the two pilots are what is called the flight crew.

Well, those few minutes dragged past like a snail, but pretty soon it was time to get on ourselves.

Well, here goes, I thought.

Poetry, who was right behind me, started to quote from John Adams's famous speech: "Sink or swim, live or die, survive or perish, I give my heart and hand to this vote . . ." From that, he swung off into a gospel chorus that was popular in our junior meeting in church:

> "Here I go in my airplane,
>   up in the air so high,
> High in my gospel airplane,
>   far up into the sky,
> Leaving the world so far below,
>   as higher and higher I go;
> You are invited to go with me,
>   up in my airplane."

The second verse starts like this: "Yes, I'll go in your airplane, up in the air so high." Then it ends with the words "I am delighted to go with you, up in your airplane."

Poetry didn't get to finish the poem, which he was actually trying to sing on his way up the portable stairway and into the plane.

"Heart, get out of my mouth!" I felt like saying because it felt as though it was there.

Inside the plane on the right was a little door leading into a room of some kind, which I afterward learned was a lavatory with running water and everything.

The plane was like a train inside, with a row of seats on each side of a narrow aisle, nice soft, cushioned seats like the ones in our new car, and a window beside each one. I followed Poetry up the aisle to where they wanted me to sit.

Soon we were all seated, with Poetry in front of me, Dragonfly behind me, and Little Jim right across the aisle. The rest of us were on one side or the other.

And then the flight crew came in, the door was shut and locked, and we were ready. I looked out my little window to watch somebody push away the portable stairway and to watch the people who were waving good-bye to us.

And there, standing just inside the gate beside my dad, was Old Man Paddler. He looked like one of the pictures I'd once seen of a man named Potato Creek Johnny, who'd lived out West in the Black Hills and had discovered the largest gold nugget ever found there.

Old Man Paddler's long white whiskers hung almost to his belt. He had a cane in his right hand, which he had to use because he was getting older and older and couldn't walk so well. I looked at my dad's big blackish-red eyebrows, and at his mustache, and at Dad himself, and swallowed something that felt stuck in my throat.

Then the big engines started to turn, first one and then the other, and the plane itself began to move. The first thing it did was to turn clear around and move slowly off on its three big balloon tires, two in front just below the place where the wings were fastened onto its body, and the other way back under the end of the tail. I'd noticed them when I was outside.

The stewardess had come through before we started and showed us how to fasten our seat belts and gave us some gum to chew. We were supposed to chew gum, so that when we got up in the air it would help our ears to keep from feeling as if they had dwarfs in them, pounding with little hammers and trying to get out.

Pretty soon our plane came to a runway. It turned left and moved faster and faster out across the field to the far end, and I expected any minute to start going up into the air. I held onto the sides of my seat, I can tell you.

But we didn't go up. Instead, when we got to the other side of the field, we stopped, and the plane turned halfway around until we were crossways on the runway. All of a sudden, the motors started to roar, first one and then the other, and the propellers went faster than a hummingbird's wings.

"Wh-what's that for?" Dragonfly asked me,

his eyes bulging a little. "What's the matter? Won't it go up?"

The plane certainly wasn't doing anything but standing still, like an automobile standing crossways on the road, and with the engines roaring.

But Poetry, who had been studying airplanes even more than I had, knew what was going on. He called back to Dragonfly and said, "They've quartered it into the wind, and they're testing the engines to see if they're all right. You wouldn't want anything to go wrong with them up in the sky, would you?"

Little Jim heard him say that, and for a minute he looked scared. Then he was grinning, even though his hands were holding onto the arms of his seat so tight the knuckles were white. I knew he wouldn't let being scared keep him from enjoying the ride.

"What's 'quartered into the wind' mean?" Dragonfly wanted to know.

"Dividing it into four equal parts," Poetry said with a sober face.

Dragonfly's eyebrows went down. He didn't feel like joking, so Poetry explained it, and Dragonfly was satisfied.

The engines must have been all right, for the plane turned the rest of the way around, and we started to move, straight into the wind, faster and faster, and the tail began to rise. Faster and faster, faster and faster.

Looking out, I saw that we weren't on the ground anymore.

4

It didn't even seem we were in an airplane—
at least it wasn't like I'd thought being in an
airplane would seem. There wasn't any sensa-
tion of being high, which a person has when he
is standing on a cliff looking down, or when he
is up in a tree along Sugar Creek and the wind
is blowing the tree back and forth.

That was because of our not having any
contact with the earth. Poetry and the book I'd
been reading said that was the reason, anyway.
It was just as if we were in a big long car, riding
on an air road that you couldn't see. Even the
noisy engines seemed quieter, because the plane
was soundproofed.

It surely was fun. As soon as we got over the
first thrill, we began to look down toward where
the people of the earth lived and to mention
different things we could see.

"We're going right straight toward Sugar
Creek," I heard Circus say.

I looked over at him, and he had on his
monkey face. He'd rather be up high in the air
than any place else, that maybe being the reason he was always climbing a tree or a barn or
something. And maybe that was why, when he
practiced the songs he was going to sing in the

Chicago church and over the radio, he'd nearly always climbed up in a tree to do it.

I sat there, feeling the safety belt across my stomach, just above my lap, looking around for a minute. Up in the front, I saw the little chrome-colored door, which was closed and on the other side of which, I knew, were two expert pilots who had probably received basic instruction in the United States Army or maybe in the Navy or Marine Corps. I knew that they were in good health, each one having to pass a physical examination every six months, like all pilots who drive planes with passengers in them.

I knew that the copilot could run the plane just as well as the pilot could, because he'd had the same training, and if anything should happen to the pilot, he could fly it himself. They were sitting side by side like two people in the front seat of a car. I knew that because I'd seen them, just before they had shut the door.

It didn't take many jiffies before we were riding over the hills above Sugar Creek. Yet it seemed we weren't even moving, we were so high. The hills looked like little anthills.

"Look!" Dragonfly exclaimed. "There's Old Man Paddler's cabin!"

It wasn't. It was the big creamery where my dad sold our cream and was ten times as big as Old Man Paddler's house with its clapboard roof.

"And there's Sugar Creek itself," Tom Till said.

It was, all right, though it looked like a little, twisted, crooked silver thread. I tried to see the swimming hole but couldn't. I did see Bumblebee Hill though, where we'd licked the stuffing out of that gang of rough boys the summer before.

In another second, it seemed—because we were moving at 400 miles an hour—we were over our town.

Dragonfly, as he nearly always does, saw something that wasn't what he thought it was. "See *there!*" he exclaimed.

I guess we nearly all forgot there were other passengers in the plane, even though we were being very quiet for a bunch of ordinarily noisy boys.

"What?" Poetry said.

"There's my mother down there waving one of Dad's big colored handkerchiefs at me."

"You're crazy," Poetry said. "That's the American flag on the top of the flagpole," which most of us agreed it was.

And then Sugar Creek was gone, and we were on our way to Chicago.

Each one of us, I noticed, had an empty sort of pint-size ice cream container right beside his seat. Dragonfly hadn't noticed his yet, and when he did, he asked what it was for.

Poetry explained by saying, "That's where you put your breakfast in case for any reason you decide you don't want it any longer."

You should have seen Dragonfly's face. Looking at him made me feel like he looked, and I could tell that he was beginning to be tired of his breakfast already.

Maybe everything would have been all right if Poetry hadn't been reminded of a story about a little boy who went to a Sunday school picnic and ate too much ice cream. Anyway, Poetry told the story.

A boy looked very sad after eating maybe seven double-dip ice cream cones.

"What's the matter?" his teacher asked him. "Didn't you get all you wanted?"

And the little fellow looked sadder still, held his stomach, and said, "I-I-I don't w-want all I g-got."

I could see that didn't help Dragonfly any. He began to look just a little pale, and I knew pretty soon he might have what is sometimes called "altitude sickness," which people on trains or in cars can get—and once in a while in an airplane—that being the reason they have empty ice cream containers beside everybody.

Even at that, Dragonfly might not have had any trouble if the plane hadn't had to make a quick climb to a higher altitude. I remembered afterward that there had been a lot of static in the control room back at the airport, which meant that not too far away there was probably an electrical storm.

You remember there had been only scattered clouds in the sky when we started. They were what is called cumulus clouds, the kind that look like the big white bundles of wool my dad gets from our sheep when we shear them in the spring. Some of them were below us and some above us, which meant we were flying about four thousand feet high. Barry Boyland had told us that, having studied clouds and knowing them the way our gang knew different kinds of shells.

No sooner had Poetry finished his story about the Sunday school boy who didn't want all the ice cream he'd had, than the pretty stewardess in the brown suit came walking up the green-rugged aisle to tell us to fasten our safety belts again, or to help us, whichever we needed.

Very quietly she announced in her very businesslike but kind voice, "We're going to climb several thousand feet to get above the storm."

What storm? I thought. I couldn't see anything but the bluest blue sky and the whitest white clouds. Of course, I couldn't see straight ahead of us as the pilots could, who had windows in front of them and all around them except for straight behind.

Barry explained it to us, while we were getting our belts fastened again and most of us were beginning to hold onto our chair arms.

He said, "The cold air of a storm is probably coming right straight toward us in a head-on collision against the warm air we've been flying in. That'll form what is called a 'storm collar,' and there will be a fierce updraft that will force those beautiful cumulus clouds upward and pack them together as tight as sardines in a can. They'll be forced into what is called a 'thunderhead.' The pilots have probably been warned from a ground station somewhere, and they are going to climb over the thunderhead."

I wasn't scared, for Barry explained it quietly and acted as if it wouldn't be any more than climbing one of the hills of Sugar Creek in a car. Then he yawned and stretched and started to read a magazine he had with him, which was a Christian magazine. Nearly all our parents were subscribers to it—except Dragonfly's—being good readers especially of that kind of literature.

Already I could tell we were beginning to climb rather fast, for my ears began to pound and to feel crazy. I chewed my gum faster and swallowed and swallowed and swallowed. But my ears kept on feeling as if there *was* a dwarf in each one, pounding with a rubber mallet and trying to get the doors open so he could get out—or else trying to get in. I couldn't tell which.

Then I looked at Dragonfly. He was very pale and was leaning over, looking pitifully at the still-empty ice cream container, which he already held in his right hand.

5

There isn't any reason I should take time to tell what happened to Dragonfly after that, and if I don't hurry up, I won't get to tell you what happened in Chicago. There was a storm, though, right after Dragonfly lost his breakfast.

We all thought he'd be all right after that, but he wasn't. He kept staying pale, and he was so dizzy he couldn't sit up, which is the same as having vertigo—a kind of swimming of the head —because we were so high.

I guess we had actually climbed to more than 20,000 feet, and that's pretty high, especially if you have to get there quick, which we did.

I was so busy myself, chewing gum and swallowing, that I hardly noticed the stewardess coming to Dragonfly with a portable oxygen apparatus. It had something that could be put on over his nose like a gas mask they use in wars, and he could breathe in all the extra oxygen he needed. He actually acted as if he had asthma. I'd seen my city cousin have it once, and it isn't fun to look at. He was actually blue in the face for a while.

But it didn't take us long to get over the thunderhead and down lower again, and that, along with the oxygen Dragonfly was getting artificially, tided him over, and he was all right again.

The funny thing was, though, after we got down lower and were cruising along, he looked around and said, "What you all looking at me so funny-like for?" which is the way people sometimes are when they've had to climb too high too fast—they can't remember much of anything about what happened while they were up there.

Barry explained it to him, and Dragonfly didn't even believe it.

"You lost your breakfast," Poetry squawked to him.

"I did not," he said, half angry. He held up an empty ice cream container to prove it, which was a new one the stewardess had brought.

Riding along in the clear blue sunlight, far above the clouds, had been a strange experience. I'd looked out the window during the storm, and there it was, away down below us, with big, black, billowing clouds, made sort of whitish too, because the sun was shining on them.

You could see lightning flashes and even hear thunder roaring. You couldn't see any of the earth at all, nothing but clouds and clouds and clouds, all moving and acting the way they do in any storm, except that I was looking *down* at them instead of up. They looked the way Sugar Creek does in the spring when it's at high flood and is spread all over the country-side, waves boiling and churning and very angry.

At last we were over Chicago, and the plane was coming down onto the big airfield there. It was a sight to see so *many* planes all around everywhere, with big mail trucks and things and a terminal ten times as big as the one we'd started from.

Pretty soon we were all walking, one at a time, down the little portable stairway and through the gate and into the terminal, where there were a big waiting room and a restaurant.

"I'm hungry," Dragonfly said the very first thing.

People were everywhere all around us, some sitting on the waiting benches, others standing and talking, and many of them in the restaurant eating.

"I'm *terribly* hungry," Dragonfly said.

And I said, "Which proves that you lost your breakfast up there in the sky."

He glared at me and denied it again, and I knew there wasn't any use to try to convince him.

Then, all of a sudden, we saw Santa Claus coming toward us. He was a big, round man with a big, round face and a big smile and a laugh that made everybody else want to laugh too.

Santa Claus, you know, is the name we'd given the jolly man we'd met up north on our camping trip, the one who'd invited Circus to come to Chicago to sing in his church and over a radio program that his church has.

Of course, none of the gang believed there

was a real Santa Claus, because our parents didn't believe in telling us there was when there wasn't, and isn't, and never was. Christmas is the time to celebrate the time when the One who made the world came down to live here for thirty-three years, and He became a little baby to begin with.

Soon some of us were in Santa's big car, and the rest of us were in a yellow-and-black taxicab, and we were all whirling along very fast through the city. It seemed even faster than being in the plane, because we were meeting other cars that were going just as fast in the other direction—and in almost every other direction —at the same time.

And then, for the first time in my life, I saw what is called an elevated train, which actually runs along on a track away up above the street. It didn't seem to have any engine to pull it but was run by electricity, and it twisted its way around above the streets and cut across corners and in between buildings, some of which were four times as high as the tallest trees along Sugar Creek.

The elevated, or El, which they called it for short, had sometimes seven or eight or even more long cars. It reminded me of my mom pushing a big needle in and out of a pair of Dad's socks that needed darning at the heels. Except that the El was like a giant needle with *joints,* some of which were bent one way and some the other, and all at the same time, threading its way between the different-sized buildings and not bumping into any of them.

Well, Dragonfly wasn't the only one of us who was hungry. The first thing Santa and Barry did was to take us all to a place called The Southern Tea Shop, which is in a very old building that was built by a man named Julian Ramsey. He used to be mayor of Chicago but is dead now. He had built the house right after the famous Chicago fire burned down his other one.

That big fire burned almost all the rest of the city at the same time. The fire had actually been started by a cow kicking over an old-fashioned lantern in a barn. When I heard that, I decided to be more careful not to let our old brindle cow do something like that to our lantern at home.

They didn't seem to have any barns in Chicago, though, and certainly not any cows. People there got their milk out of bottles, which grew on their front porch steps every morning. Of course they didn't *actually,* but anybody who could believe in Santa Claus could believe that too.

Well, there we were in the tea shop, all sitting around neat little tables. Over in a corner near a big window, standing on a radiator, I think it was, was a bright, funny-looking brass thing that I knew my mom would like to see, because she was always interested in what is called "antiques." We found out it was an old Russian teakettle, which had a place for burning charcoal to get the water hot. Of course, nobody used it anymore.

After waiting far too long for Dragonfly to wait any longer, our dinner was carried in. Mmmm! Southern fried chicken and hot biscuits, all we could eat! A waitress wearing a white apron and white cap kept going from table to table, bringing more biscuits or water or whatever people wanted.

You can believe me that I was glad my parents had made me read a book on etiquette, which tells how to eat with good manners. Even though I didn't always remember to have 100 percent good manners at our table at home, I would have been terribly embarrassed not to know how to eat in a fancy place like that.

I felt very sorry for Tom Till. He didn't know which spoon to take first, the one on the right or the left of the three or four we had. But he was a smart little guy. I watched him out of the corner of my eye, and whenever he didn't know how to do something, he looked out of the corner of *his* eye to see how the rest of us were doing it, and then he'd do it the same way. And do you know what? Tom was watching me more than he was any of the rest of us, and I felt proud to think I could set a good example for him.

All the time, though, he was using another corner of his eye to look at the people who walked past the window outside. There was a sad expression on his face, which meant maybe he was thinking of his brother, Bob, who might be in Chicago somewhere. Whenever he saw a policeman or saw a patrol car go past, he looked bothered.

After dinner, we all went to a YMCA. After resting a while, we went swimming in water that was clean all the way to the bottom. After that, we sat around in a sort of club room and made plans for doing different things. There would be time to do only a dozen or more important things—not nearly all we'd planned when we were at home.

For Little Jim's sake, we decided to let him ride on an escalator. Besides that, we'd have time to visit the famous Field Museum, and the Planetarium, and the stockyards, and Chinatown, and we could ride to different places on the El.

When Sunday came, we were going to visit a jail where there would be boys who hadn't been trained up in the way they ought to go. We'd all give our testimonies there, and Circus would sing. When Santa mentioned "jail," I looked sideways at Tom.

He swallowed, and his freckled face turned red, but he didn't say a word.

Later on that first day, we would go to a rescue mission where we'd see a lot of *men* who had grown up not having been trained in the way they should have gone.

We decided on Little Jim's escalator first and got that over with. (Wow, there were more people in that one store than lived in all Sugar Creek.) It was fun to walk up to a stairway, right out in the middle of a big store, and see the stairway slowly going up—all the steps moving at once—and right beside it another stairway, coming down, each step disappearing the minute it got to the bottom. People would come down on it not even walking but just getting on a step and standing there!

Just for fun, most of us rode up and down either behind or directly in front of Little Jim. It was while Little Jim and I were alone once that he showed what kinds of thoughts were riding up and down in his curly head most of the time. I was on the step right behind him, and my red head was just as high as his brown one was. In fact, my hand was on his shoulder.

"Know what this reminds me of?" he asked in my ear.

"What?" I said.

"Of the story in the Bible about Jacob's dream."

I remembered the story. My parents had it in a Bible storybook, which they saw to it that I read regularly instead of a lot of murder stories in comic books. But that doesn't belong to this story.

I kept on riding up the escalator with Little Jim, and then at the top we got on the one going down and went down for the last time. Barry wouldn't let us ride more than a few times, since escalators were not made to be played on.

Little Jim knew I was interested in things about the Bible, so he was always waiting for a chance to tell me his thoughts. In that short minute on the way down, he said, "It reminds me of the story of the ladder Jacob saw in his dream. It reached up to heaven, and there were angels going up and down on it."

Well, I looked over Little Jim's shoulder to the gang waiting for us at the bottom of the escalator—red-haired, freckle-faced Tom Till; Circus with his messed-up hair and monkey face; Poetry, as round as a barrel and mischievous; Dragonfly, with a nose that turned south at the end and eyes too big for his little face; and Big Jim, who had shaved off his mustache especially for the Chicago trip and would probably have to shave again before Christmas.

"What angels?" I asked Little Jim, looking skeptically at the Sugar Creek Gang, which certainly didn't look like angelic beings.

We got to the bottom then and didn't have a chance to finish what we were talking about, not until we were in the Planetarium.

The big room where the planetarium machine sat was round and seated hundreds of people. In the center was the craziest-looking man-made thing I ever saw, looking like a skeleton with two heads, one at each end, and with eyes all over it. It also reminded me of a giant caterpillar, ten feet long and more than a foot thick, with two heads and with eyes on both ends and everywhere. Or maybe a very large ant.

All of a sudden, while we were sitting there, the sky, which at first had looked like a big cement dome, began to get dark. At the same time, a lady with a very pleasant voice began explaining to us all about the astronomy of the thing, using more words and bigger than I knew the dictionary had.

Before long, stars began to come out in the dome. The "caterpillar" was throwing the stars up there, yet you couldn't see any lights on the caterpillar at all, only on the sky. The next thing we knew, it was all dark, with stars all over the sky. It was just the way it is at night along Sugar Creek, only there weren't any mosquitoes.

It was a wonderful sight, with the stars all moving around in different directions. There was a moon and sometimes a sun, and different planets, which I'd read about somewhere, such as Jupiter and Saturn. Saturn looked like a white baseball with some of my mom's white yarn wrapped around it, making what is called a "ring." Or like a wide-brimmed white hat.

There were maybe a zillion things to see in the Planetarium, but it was when we were in the auditorium under that artificial sky with a million stars in it that Little Jim remembered and finished what he wanted to say.

While we were sitting there in the dark, his hand reached across the arm of his chair and got hold of mine. He leaned over and asked a question. "Jacob's ladder reached clear up into heaven, didn't it?"

I whispered back, "Sure. Why?"

Do you know what he had been thinking? He said, "I think that ladder was supposed to represent Jesus, who is the only way to heaven there is, and we can all go up on Him, and we can all go to heaven free if we have Him. All we have to do is to get on and ride, which is maybe the same as being saved by grace."

Imagine that little guy thinking that all out by himself!

Just that minute, the whole sky began to move around in a strange circle. Some stars went one way and some another, all going in different directions. The big black ant out in the middle of the auditorium was slowly turning over on its side and twisting around at the same time.

For a minute, the thoughts in my head started going around just like the stars were, so it wasn't until afterward that I remembered a Bible verse that proved Little Jim was right, which he nearly always is.

The only thing wrong with the pretty lady's very interesting talk was that she didn't mention God as having had anything to do with creating the heavens and the earth, as the Bible says.

Barry explained that to us later, having been graduated from a genuinely Christian college and knowing all about astronomy and where the stars came from.

As I said, I didn't get to decide whether Little Jim was right until afterward, which was that same night when we were away down in the slums of the city where there was a famous rescue mission.

Most of us would get the surprise of our

lives that night. I'll have to say, I guess there never was such an experience just waiting to happen to a boy.

None of us expected to see Big Bob Till in the Pacific Garden Mission.

6

Right after we left the planetarium and before we had supper, which is called *dinner* in Chicago, we took a long, winding walk through the Field Museum. I'm glad we went there before going to the mission.

I'll explain why in just a minute.

I'd rather have gone to the zoo to see if maybe Little Jim's bear was there, but the museum was close to the Planetarium, so we went there right away. While Barry and Santa Claus were taking us through, explaining different things to us, I couldn't help but think we were sort of like the twelve disciples following, except that there were only seven of us.

The Field Museum has the largest and the most wonderful collection of what are called "specimens" in the whole world—animal and mineral and vegetable, Barry said.

I wrote down a few notes about things he told me afterward, and this is what he said: "The exhibits of the Field Museum are divided into four categories—anthropology, or the science of mankind; botany, or the science of plants; zoology, or the science of animals; and geology, the science of minerals." Sometime I'll know more about these things.

Well, we walked along what is called Stanley

Hall, which is the main passageway of the whole thing, kind of like the midway in a dead circus. The first thing we saw was two fierce-looking dead elephants standing as though they were alive and wanted to fight. I could tell that Circus wished he could shinny right up the leg of one of them the way he does a tree along Sugar Creek and then swing around on one of the elephants' trunks and get up on top.

Poetry started in right away with a poem, which went:

"I went to the animal fair,
    The birds and the beasts were there,
The gay baboon by the light of the moon
    Was combing his auburn hair."

That made me think of my dad with his reddish-brownish-blackish mustache and his long shaggy eyebrows. I could see him with my mind's eyes, standing in our bathroom before the mirror, combing his eyebrows the way he does sometimes. Mom teases him about it.

Poetry rattled on with the poem and finally ended with nobody paying much attention to him:

"Then just as the clock struck nine,
    The animals formed a line;
First came the monk on the elephant's trunk,
    And invited him down to dine."

The different animals we saw were all stuffed

with something that made them look the way they were when they were alive. I think the name of the business that stuffs and mounts animals is "taxidermy."

Many animals were shown in settings that were just like the kind they lived in when they were alive. Some were from America, some from Africa, some from Asia. There were also a lot of skeletons of many different kinds of animals.

We even saw a big water hole, which wasn't actual water, and a lot of animals by it. "Mammals" Barry called them. A mammal is any kind of an animal that has a backbone and whose mother feeds it the same way old Mixy-cat feeds her little kittens.

Poetry counted twenty-three mammals all ranged around the African water hole. Several of them were tall giraffes, and one was a rhinoceros with a little bird on its back.

And then we were past the animals and in the botany department, which didn't interest us so much, except that it showed how much human beings depend on plants for enough to eat.

Then we went to the anthropology part of the museum. It was interesting to see the different people of the world living in the same way they do or used to or, anyway, the way they were supposed to have lived when they were alive.

Once Little Tom stood still, looking at some people who were like people in Tibet, and all of a sudden he said, "Are all those different people just stuffed dead people, like the animals back there?"

Imagine that!

"Of course not!" Poetry said, astonished.

Even Dragonfly looked across the top of his crooked nose and said, "Of course not! They made them out of plaster of paris or something and painted them the different colors!" which was the right answer.

In the geology section, we saw skeletons of curious animals that were supposed to have lived many millions of years ago. I was glad that when I am at home and running lickety-sizzle through the woods toward Sugar Creek, I don't have to be afraid a great big log will suddenly turn out to be a dinosaur's long tail that will swish around and knock me all to smithereens.

Over in another section, the name of which I can't remember, we stopped in front of an eagle's nest. It was about four feet across and was made of sticks and twigs with some soft material in the middle. Right in the center were several baby eagles, which were as big as our old red rooster at home and had fuzz all over them.

Above the nest was the baby eagles' great big mom with fierce-looking eyes and with wings that would measure about six feet from tip to tip. Clutched in her cruel, long talons was a snowshoe rabbit, which the mother was going to tear up in a minute and feed to her hungry babies.

While we were all looking at the eagle's

nest and at the white rabbit in the mother's talons, we listened to Barry explain that baby eagles were very stubborn when they got old enough to fly. They wouldn't get out of the nest and try their wings, so the mother bird had to stir up the nest and almost push them off the edge of the cliff.

I looked around to see if that had given Little Jim any ideas, and he was looking up at that rabbit dangling there, and there were tears in his eyes. He saw me looking at him, and as he always does when tears get in his eyes, he turned his head and shook it a little. When I saw his eyes again, the tears were gone and were lying somewhere on the marble floor of the museum. As many times in my life as I've seen Little Jim cry, I've never seen him use his handkerchief to get rid of his tears.

"'S'matter?" I asked him on the side.

"N-nothing," he gulped back to me. Then he said, "It's a pretty rabbit, isn't it? It looks like a lamb."

When he said that, I knew that maybe in his mind he was spelling the word *lamb* with a capital L and maybe was thinking about the best Friend a boy ever had, the One who had been called the "Lamb of God who takes away the sin of the world."

After looking at the eagles, we crossed over and saw some birds that are called rhinoceros hornbills. There were two of them, one on the outside of a tree trunk and the other on the inside, with only its big twelve-inch-long bill sticking out of a small hole. We found out that the one on the outside was the dad and the one on the inside was the mom, and that all daddy hornbills always shut up their wives inside a hollow tree and plaster the hole shut except for a very small opening. The mother has to stay inside all the time she is sitting on the nest until the baby hornbills are hatched and so big they crowd her out.

"You'd think she'd starve to death in there," Poetry said. "Boy! I'm hungry!"

"Starve?" Big Jim said. "Listen to this . . ." And he read the explanation that was printed on a sign on the display cage.

And do you know what? That daddy bird with his yellowish bill, as long as a cow's horn, not only carried mud and stuff and plastered up the hole so his wife couldn't get out—and so that monkeys and other animals couldn't get in to destroy the nest, and maybe so his wife would be sure to stay at home and look after the children—but he actually worked hard all day long for weeks to find food for her to eat.

Well, I thought, as we all scrambled on to the next exhibit, *hornbills are very interesting.*

When we walked out of the museum, watching the hundreds of people walking past or standing on the steps, we could see Lake Michigan, which wasn't far away. Then we went down a very wide sidewalk and through a tunnel under the street and out on the other side, where we all bought some ice cream.

The famous Shedd Aquarium was next. At the entrance, I looked up at the big electric light, and it had on it a huge starfish carved in stone or iron or something for decoration.

Inside the mammoth-sized aquarium building there were people and people and people, and fish and fish and fish of every kind and shape and color of the rainbow. *Live* fish, all of them! Big, little, long, short, flat, pug-nosed, stumpy-tailed, round, with horns, without them, all swimming, each kind in its own private aquarium. It was a sight to see and made me wish I could just once catch one of them on my fishing pole in Sugar Creek.

From the aquarium we walked on a high cement fence along the lakefront—and shouldn't have, maybe. A long, wide, and high cement something-or-other ran out like a bent elbow far into the lake. It was called a "breakwater" and was supposed to protect the shore from the terrible force of the waves, especially if there should ever be a windstorm. There were maybe a thousand sea gulls on and off it.

Well, we all wanted to take a ride in a speedboat, and we did. Wow! That was a thrill! Our boat shot out across the water and around to the other side of the breakwater, where the waves were high and where the spray dashed over the gunwale and made a lot of beautiful little rainbows, so close to us that I reached out and stuck my arm into the one that was flying right along with us.

Then, just for fun, Poetry took both hands

and clasped them together and said, "Here, Bill, have a chunk of rainbow."

I reached out and took it and ate it.

We squealed and hollered and laughed and got a little frightened, especially Little Jim. He had his eyes focused on the edge of the rainbow, and I knew he maybe had one in his mind too. He was grinning and holding onto Big Jim, and I heard him say, "It's nice to have a rainbow flying right along beside you."

And if I'd been a preacher or a minister, I'll bet I could have thought up something interesting for my congregation next Sunday morning.

After the ride, we walked along the waterfront and felt the cool breeze fanning our cheeks. Then we came to the boulevard. We would have walked over to the Conrad Hilton Hotel, which as I told you was the largest hotel in the world, but the traffic was so fast and so heavy that Barry and Santa made us walk all the way back to the tunnel that went under the street.

It was a long walk, past the museum again and over a high wooden bridge with a lot of railroad tracks under it and the trains flying along under there every few minutes. Ahead were the great high buildings of the city, looking like tall, irregular lower teeth in some fierce wild animal's mouth.

Soon we were at the hotel and were inside, where we were supposed to write cards or letters to our folks to tell them we had arrived in Chicago without being scared to death. I wrote a *long* letter to my folks and told them all I could think of about the city.

Poetry, who is an expert in arithmetic, remember, and who is also mischievous, helped me write the letter, and this is what I wrote:

Dear Mom and Dad
and pug-nosed Charlotte Ann,

I am now sitting at a desk in the world's largest hotel, a picture of which you will see on the postcard enclosed. Actually, I didn't know such a hotel existed.

There are 2,600 guest rooms in it, and if the seven members of the Sugar Creek Gang would decide to sleep in all of them one night at a time, each one of us having his own room, it would take all of us over a year and a month to do it. If I wanted to sleep in every one of them myself, it would take me more than eight years, and by that time I would have slept on sixty freight-car loads of innerspring mattresses.

The dining rooms are so big that when they first bought enough plates for them, they had to buy 134,000, besides 50 carloads of other chinaware, enough to fill all the silos on maybe 25 farms around Sugar Creek. I could use 3 napkins a day, and it would take me over 273 years to use all of them.

They have 138,000 tablecloths, and if all their 48,000 drinking glasses were filled with water at the same time and poured out in Sugar Creek all at once, it might cause a flood! They have enough silverware to fill our haymow twice. If you want to come here sometime, you can not only check your suitcases and come back for them, but you can check Charlotte Ann, and they'll keep her till you come back.

Not only that, but one long street in this town, Western Avenue, is as long as from Sugar Creek to Sandville, which, as you know, is twenty-four miles. They have thousands of firemen in the fire department, and they surely need them because it seems every few minutes I hear a fire engine going past.

Poetry is sitting right beside me at the table in this very beautiful room, reading about the Chicago River in a book. He says it is one of the few rivers in the world that flows backward. That is, instead of flowing toward its *mouth*, the *way* any decent river should, it goes the other way.

Well, this letter will have to close because tonight we are all going down on South State Street to a famous rescue mission, where many years ago a baseball player named Billy Sunday was converted. He was a famous evangelist and is dead now. Some people who became very important in the Christian world were born again at that mission. One of them, Barry told us, was named Mel Trotter, and he went to Grand Rapids, Michigan, and founded what became the largest city rescue mission in the world.

In fact, I have to stop writing right now, because first we have to make a visit to the Moody Bible Institute, which is the largest Bible school in the world and where Circus has to practice singing before a microphone, with Little Jim playing for him, so he won't be so frightened when he actually sings over the radio.

I am having a wonderful time, which I'll tell you about when I get home, especially about the airplane trip. Here we go now to Moody Bible Institute!

Wonderfully yours,
Bill

7

A nd that night we saw Bob Till.
It was while we were at the rescue mission, though, and we didn't get there until after supper, which we ate at the Moody Bible Institute.

Thousands and thousands of young people have been trained there to be missionaries, pastors, teachers, choir directors, evangelists, and Christian education directors.

We went downstairs with Barry and Santa Claus—whose real name I ought to tell you is the Reverend Don Farmer—and pretty soon we were standing in front of our plates at a long table in the school dining room. All around us were hundreds and hundreds of people, nearly all young people, and everybody was talking and laughing and smiling until some soft chimes sounded. Then somebody started a song, which was a church hymn tune, using the words

> Be present at our table, Lord,
>   Be here and everywhere adored;
>   These mercies bless, and grant that we
>   May feast in paradise with Thee.

It was the first time I'd ever thought about there being something good to eat when we got to heaven, and I thought it was a good idea because I was terribly hungry right that minute. So also was Poetry, who was always hungry anyway, and so also was Dragonfly, who had digested only one meal that day.

In a few seconds, there was a scraping of about one thousand chairs as one thousand people in that great big dining room sat down and waited to be served. Again I was glad I knew my manners and not only knew them but had had sense enough to practice them at home so I didn't look awkward in a public place like that.

But pretty soon supper was over, and the one thousand people started getting up from the different tables and going out. Upstairs, in what was called the lobby, we met a lot of different people, such as the president of the school, and the dean of men, and the director of the radio department where Circus was going to sing, and where in a few minutes he was going to practice.

Rooms, rooms, rooms, people, people, people, and nearly everybody was carrying a Bible under his arm or in his hand, just the way children carry their schoolbooks. I reached into my vest pocket and took out my own little thin New Testament and carried it out where people could see that I wasn't ashamed of it.

Then we went to the administration building and into an elevator. All of us crowded in with Barry and Santa Claus—Mr. Farmer—all of us taking off our different kinds of hats or caps, whichever we'd worn, because there was a lady on the elevator too.

Up, up we went, stopping at every floor to see if there was anybody else who wanted to get on. But soon we were away up in a little room in the radio tower, and Circus and Little Jim were ready to practice.

The piano was what is called a baby grand, and it surely looked nice. The round microphone, which stood on a long brasslike stem, looked kind of like a small steering wheel on a car. Circus had learned his song by heart, and so had Little Jim, which is the way to make a song sound better when you're singing it, and so that, if people are watching you sing, you can look them right in the eyes and make them listen better.

None of us knew, of course, that Santa— Mr. Farmer—had a surprise planned for us that night in his apartment. But that comes later.

Moody Bible Institute, we found out, is not only the largest Bible institute in the world, but their radio is dedicated, as Old Man Paddler will be very glad to know, "wholly to the service of the Lord Jesus Christ."

Before we left there that night to go to the mission, they handed us some literature telling about the school, which I sent home to my mom and dad, and Poetry sent home to his parents.

I could just see my mom and dad sitting at our kitchen table, with Charlotte Ann in her high chair beside them, and nobody sitting at my place. I'll bet they'd have my chair there, though, and maybe my plate and my favorite blue mug out of which I drank milk three times a day.

And Dad would open my letter from Chicago and read it, and then he'd say, "Wow! Look at this about the Moody Bible Institute! It says there are thousands of people who study the Bible by *mail* from there!"

Then my mom might lean over, and they'd read it together, with his bushy red hair and her brownish-gray hair brushing against each other. And they'd read about the teachers, and the more than one thousand students, and the library, and the evening school, and the magazine, and the school's radio station, and all the former students who have gone to be missionaries in countries around the world.

My parents would also be glad to know that Little Jim had already made up his mind he wanted to go to school there sometime.

As soon as Little Jim and Circus finished practicing, we all went over to what was called the "153 Building" and up to a room called "Mr. Moody's Room," where they had different things about Dwight L. Moody's life—the man who started the school in the first place. There were a lot of things to see, such as a chair they wouldn't let anybody sit in, because it was Mr. Moody's old chair.

To me the most interesting thing was a picture of a gang of fourteen ragged-looking boys who belonged to Mr. Moody's first Sunday school many years ago. They were sitting or half sitting or standing, and one of them had a worn-out broom in front of him.

"What crazy names," Poetry said, reading some of them out loud.

Each boy's strange name was printed right below his picture. I listened to Poetry's squawky voice calling off the ridiculous names, and this is what some of them were: "Red Eye, Smikes, Butcher, Rag Breeches . . ." Rag Breeches was the one who had the broom.

Right above the gang of boys was printed "BEFORE," which means the way the boys looked when Mr. Moody got them to start to Sunday school.

Then, right beside that picture was another picture of the same gang of boys, and they had their hair combed and had on new suits, which some rich Christian in Chicago had paid for. The boys earned the suits by going to Sunday school quite a while. There was certainly a difference in the looks of the two pictures.

All of a sudden, Little Tom Till, who was standing at my right elbow, piped up and said, "What happened to the *other two?*"

"What other two?" I said, and then I looked, and sure enough he was right. On the first picture, the one called "BEFORE," there were fourteen boys. On the picture entitled "AFTER," there were only twelve.

"Maybe they stopped going to Sunday school," Little Jim said.

And my mind went off wondering what

became of those two extra boys, and what kind of parents they had. I hoped none of our gang would ever stop going to Sunday school and drop out of the picture.

Soon after that we were on a bus going to the mission. Circus and I sat together. The rest of us were on one side or the other. A lot of different-looking people were all around and in front of us and behind us, and I thought that if anybody wanted to be a missionary and for some reason didn't get to go to a foreign country, he could be one right in Chicago.

All of a sudden, Little Jim got up out of his seat and balanced himself, holding onto the seat tops. Then he staggered forward two or three seats and handed a piece of paper to a little boy who was sitting there beside his mom. I knew it was a gospel tract.

Little Jim acted very bashful while he slipped back to his seat beside Santa Claus, he being the only one of us who could actually sit beside him without having to put a foot out into the aisle to keep from falling off. Well, now, maybe that statement was what is called exaggeration, but Santa, or Mr. Farmer, is a very big man, anyway.

At last there we were, just about two blocks, which we would have to walk, from the mission. I guess I never saw so many people in my life who looked like they were prodigal sons and who ought to go back home and get cleaned up, as well as confess their sins and get their souls washed.

We walked along the way people do in cities, everybody walking very fast and in a terrible hurry to get somewhere from somewhere—not at all like people do in Sugar Creek, who know they are alive and that the world isn't going to fall to pieces tomorrow.

Down those two blocks, all along the sidewalk, were some filthy-looking theaters and old saloons. And everywhere were electric signs doing all kinds of things, whirling in circles, jabbing back and forth like arrows, zigzagging like a football player dodging through a crowd of other players, blinking on and off and on and off without ever stopping. Most of the signs advertised beer or liquor or cheap rooms.

And then we were there, getting a drink out of a bubbling little water fountain just outside the mission door.

In the window of the mission, which was like a big long store building, was a sign asking, "How Long Since You Wrote to Mother?" There was also a big Bible, wide open, with a verse marked for people to read.

Poetry was already reading the verse out loud in his squawky voice, which was half boy's voice and half man's. It was the verse that begins, "I will get up and go to my father, and will say unto him, 'Father, I have sinned . . .'"

Just inside the door, a smiling man handed us a hymnbook, which was the same kind we used in our church at home. Then the superintendent, a tall, smiling, big-voiced man, led us all the way up the long aisle to the front, up the platform stairs, which looked freshly polished, and across the platform, on each side of which was a big grand piano. He took us into an office in the back where there was a man at a desk. We left our different kinds of caps there.

Santa had us all sit down in the office. He was going to preach at the mission that night, and some of the men of his church were going to give their testimonies, his church being the kind of a church that was alive enough to have what is called a gospel team, like the one our church has at Sugar Creek and which my dad is the leader of.

There was a prayer meeting in the office before we began the mission meeting itself, and all of us got down on our knees with the superintendent and Barry and Santa.

Then, up we got and out we went, and pretty soon we were sitting on the platform between the two big pianos. I wished Little Jim could have played one of them, but they already had a man sitting on each piano bench, and I knew Little Jim would have to wait until Circus's solo before he would get to play.

It would take too long to tell *every* interesting thing that happened, so I'll skip some of it. But, of course, I felt proud of Little Jim while he played the piano for Circus's song.

Circus's voice sounded even sweeter than when he was singing from a treetop along Sugar Creek. It was really wonderful. His brown hair glistened under the big electric light above his head, and the people out in the long audience acted as though they couldn't move and didn't want to anyway.

I always liked to sit on a platform and look out at all the different people's different kinds of faces, the way I do at a big herd of cattle in a field, which stand still and look at you if you happen to have on a red sweater.

I never will forget what the superintendent said when Circus finished. He stood there very straight for a bit after Circus had sat down, and then he said to the people, "It's unusual to see a fine boy like this using his voice for the Lord, instead of singing the music of the world."

He turned to Circus and made him stand beside him. Then he put his arm halfway around him the way my dad does me when he likes me or is proud of me for something, and he said to the people, "How many of you will promise to pray for this young man, that God will make him a mighty power in the world for winning souls?"

I looked at Circus through the superintendent's eyes, and he actually looked like a young man. Then I looked at myself through my own eyes, and I didn't look like very much—only a redheaded kid with too many freckles, and I wasn't growing fast enough.

Well, in answer to the superintendent's question, I saw nearly every hand in the crowd go up—the hands of the nice-looking people who were there to visit the mission, and even some of the dirty, wrinkled-up hands of some of the drunks and of the other men. Some men had been half asleep, and some had just been hushed up for talking out loud in church.

Pacific Garden Mission had what was called a "formal service," but the people acted like a great big family, and sometimes they were even noisy. Still, it seemed all the Christian people there loved God with all their hearts. Over on the right side of the room and about halfway back sat three rows of young people who had come from some church in Chicago to visit and to give their testimonies when it was time for them to do it.

Then, all of a sudden, right in the middle of the testimony meeting, a man stood up right under the big picture of Billy Sunday, which was hanging on the wall over the heads of the young people. With a loud, gruff, and very husky voice he started to tell everybody what a terrible drunk he had once been. He had tried to quit drinking for many years and couldn't. "And then, one night," he said, "when I was about to kill myself and was staggering around on the street, I heard music, which was coming right through that door there and . . ."

Talk about being glad he was saved! That man certainly sounded like it. In fact, he waved his arms and walked out into the aisle. He reminded me of a man in a prizefight. He had a crooked nose that was also flat, and, in fact, I learned he *had* been a prizefighter once.

The next man who talked looked like a very important businessman, with pretty white hair and a good shave. He talked quietly and very kindly.

It was when they were taking the collection, or rather when *we* were that we saw Bob Till come in at the door and sit down on a back seat. I say "we" were taking the offering, because the superintendent asked two of the Sugar Creek Gang to do it. He looked around at us, who were sitting behind him, and picked out Big Jim and me and handed us the offering plates, which looked like two of my mom's new, bright tin baking pans.

I'd never helped take an offering before, so I felt a little embarrassed at first but proud too. We started at the front and were working our way to the rear—most people not giving anything because many of them didn't have anything to give; some had just come in so they could have a place to sleep that night.

I didn't have more than seventy-five cents in my offering pan—and I was almost to the back of the room—when all of a sudden I looked, and there was a ten-dollar bill in it, which a drunken man had dropped in. Most drunken men are nearly always glad to give their money away or else drink it up or buy drinks for anybody else who wants them.

And right that minute the door opened, and Bob Till staggered in. I couldn't believe my eyes, and yet there he was, slithering into a seat in a corner right in front of me. I was still taking the offering and was facing the door, so I could see him. He sort of melted down into his seat and ducked his head.

8

You could have knocked me over with an exclamation point, I was so surprised to see him there. I leaned over and whispered, "Hi, Bob!"

Bob Till's head shot up.

The two pianos on the platform were playing a duet, with somebody accompanying them on a violin, so nobody but us could hear what we said to each other.

And I guess you could have knocked *him* over with a comma or maybe a period. He turned white. He stared at me and then at the money in the offering plate, looking as if he had seen a red-haired, freckle-faced ghost. He didn't actually look very much like himself, though. His face was dirty, and his hair was combed on a different side and at the same time looked messed up the way mine does when I've been standing on my head in our front yard at home.

"Shh!" Bob said. "Don't tell anybody who I am. The police . . ." He slid down farther into his seat, grabbed a songbook, and buried his face in it.

And for some reason I began to feel very sorry for Big Bob Till. Anyway, I was sorry for his brother, Tom, so I kept still.

Big Jim hadn't even noticed him, so we walked back up to the platform with our offering plates and sat down again and watched the meeting. The more I looked back to the row where Bob Till was, the more I realized that he didn't look like himself at all. Maybe I was the only one of the gang who would recognize him, I thought.

But just that minute, I felt Poetry nudge me in the side, and he said, "Look who's in the back row!"

"Shh!" I said and glanced out the corner of my eye at Little Tom. I really didn't know what to do. I wondered why Bob was staying in the meeting when he knew we were there.

Poetry whispered to me again. "I'll bet he doesn't know we know about the stolen money from Mr. Simondson's grocery, or he'd beat it out into the street and hide somewhere."

I hadn't thought of that. Of course, he didn't know, I thought, so I kept on keeping still, and the meeting went on to its close.

Well, I'd seen people take their suitcases into railroad depots or into hotels and check them and get a little round card called a "check" with a number on it, then come back later and hand the card to the baggage man and get back the suitcases. But I'd never heard of a man taking *himself* to a mission and checking *himself* in, but that's exactly what happened.

Pretty soon there began a slow parade of sad-faced men walking past us to the platform. Each one took a little round check with a number on it and crossed the platform to the stair door.

Such men I'd never seen before or even read about. I mean such unhappy men. It really was a terrible sight to see—all kinds of men with all kinds of shaped heads and different-length, different-colored hair, all of it needing to be washed and also their faces.

They all had different kinds of eyes too. Some were bleary, some were just sad, and there wasn't a one that had a twinkle in it. Some of the men looked very fierce. Some were slouched over and acted as though they wished they weren't alive—which Dad says is the way anybody feels who doesn't have any hope. Only a few of them looked as if they were actually alive in their souls.

Thinking about that made me wonder why anybody ever wanted to hire out to the devil in the first place, if that was the kind of wages he paid all his hired men.

And then I saw Bob Till coming. He had his hair pulled down over his eyes and his shirt collar turned up about his neck. His head was down. He glanced at Big Jim, and at the same time, I looked down and saw Bob's fists double up, and I knew he hated Big Jim.

I looked quick at the rest of our gang, and Poetry was the only one who had recognized Bob. Even Tom didn't know him.

Then Bob had his check and was up on the platform, following the others. I watched until he was gone upstairs. I looked around, and none of the gang looked as if they'd seen any-body they knew.

About six minutes later, we were allowed to go upstairs to watch the men go to bed. Barry and Mr. Farmer—Santa—went up with us and also one of the workers of the mission. It was not only interesting to see, but it was absolutely the unhappiest thing I ever saw. Not a man was smiling, and nobody acted glad he was alive.

The man who had given them their checks was up there too, going from one cot to anoth-er, getting their names and putting each name down beside the number of his check. Men, men, men, all over.

"I don't think that's Bob after all," Poetry said to me.

I looked again and decided maybe Poetry was right.

Just before we left, the man who'd been taking names stopped at one of the cots and said to the man lying there, "Hey, buddy, put your head down at *this* end!"

I didn't like that. I thought a man had a right to put his head at whichever end of the bed he wanted to, but Barry explained it. "The law says that they have to sleep so they can't breathe or cough in any other man's face. That's a health law."

And then I understood.

I thought about my nice soft mattress at home in our upstairs, and the cool clean sheets, and of my neat mom who always had my bed turned down for me at night, and for a minute

I couldn't see straight. Some crazy old tears kept getting mixed up in my eyes.

I looked at Little Jim, and I saw him turn his face away and give his curly head a toss, and I knew that somewhere on that wooden floor would be a couple of tears.

Soon we were all going down the stairs to the main floor and out onto the street. We were going to Santa's apartment, where at midnight he had a very strange surprise waiting for us.

We stopped at the mission door, though, and they let us look over the list of names of the men who were upstairs. And would you believe it? There were five men who had the same name, and that name was "Frank Smith."

"Who *are* they?" Dragonfly asked. "Are they all brothers or what?"

"Nobody knows who they are," the mission man said. "We get a lot of men by that name."

There was even a man named John Doe on the list. I let my eye slide down the whole page, and there wasn't anybody there named Bob Till, either, so I knew if it really *was* Bob, he had given a false name.

Outside the mission we all stopped to get a drink at the little drinking fountain. The Chicago water didn't taste as good to me as the water from the spring at Sugar Creek.

When I looked up from getting my drink, a police car was parking right in front of the mission. Two big burly policemen climbed out and walked up to the door. They gave us boys a careful looking over, then they went into the mission, and we went on to Santa's apartment, each one of us thinking his own thoughts.

On the way, we went through a part of the city called Chinatown, where many Chinese people lived and where I bought a pound of tea. I asked the Chinese clerk to wrap it up and send it to my mom, who liked Chinese tea very much.

In another store, we saw a half-dozen men sitting around a table. Each one had a little pile of money in front of him, and they were playing some kind of game using small yellow cubes with Chinese characters on them. The cubes looked like little pieces of cream cheese. In another store, a man was mixing perfume. In still another, we saw a Chinese paper dragon, as long as our barn at home. It was all-colored and looked like a big rainbow that had been straightened out, except that it had a fierce head with savage eyes.

We couldn't stay long in Chinatown, but it surely was an interesting place. Once I saw a cute, mischievous-looking, black-haired Chinese boy on the sidewalk. Some tourists were standing around in a little half circle, watching him and laughing at things he said and did. His mom, who was very pretty, was watching him too and acting proud, just as my mom does when people look at Charlotte Ann and tell Mom how cute she is.

In the car, on the way to Santa's apartment, Santa said, "You ought to visit our Chinese Sunday school sometime. We have over fifty teachers, one teacher for every student."

They talked about that a while, but Poetry and I still had our thoughts on Bob Till. We wondered to each other what those police officers wanted to go into the mission for.

We would find out Sunday morning when we went to visit a boys' jail.

9

At Santa's apartment we had our strange surprise, and Little Jim taught me another important lesson.

Mrs. Santa, or really Mrs. Farmer—I was learning to call her that—met us with a smile and a gurgling giggle that was very cheerful. She introduced us to their canary, Cheery, which was trained and could be let out of the cage and would fly around from room to room. It would stand on a dresser in front of a mirror and act very angry at its reflection, not knowing maybe that it was seeing only its very pretty yellow self.

All over the apartment were cots for us to sleep on. Santa's study had two cots in it as well as a library.

Mrs. Farmer seemed as tickled to see all of us as if we had been her own boys, which, just for fun, she said we were. She had sandwiches ready for us and gave each of us a glass of milk.

After a half hour or more, we all got ready for bed. It was funny to see us decked out in our different colored pajamas, ready to climb into our cots. Poetry's pajamas were white with reddish-purple stripes running around them, which made him look like a prisoner from some jail. We would have teased the life out of him if we hadn't all remembered Bob Till and felt sorry for little red-haired Tom, so that joke was spoiled.

Pretty soon we sang a chorus and said our prayers, each one saying his own quietly beside his own bed. Then we climbed in, and the lights went out.

I was certainly tired. Dragonfly was in a cot beside me in the study, but I went right off to sleep and into a crazy dream with things scrambling around in my mind—canaries and stars and dinosaurs and dragons and fish.

I was dreaming I'd turned into a giant-sized needle and was darning Dad's socks, when I was awakened by somebody at the window, standing out there on the fire escape and dressed in a striped prison suit.

Well, it didn't make sense and was part of my dream, I thought, so I didn't believe it—not until whoever it was began to rattle the window and to crawl inside, the screen having been taken off already.

Dragonfly woke up scared, and pretty soon everybody in all the rooms was awake. The lights were turned on, and it was Poetry himself.

"Just a new way to wake people up," he said. He stood there in our room and yawned and acted indifferent until Dragonfly decided to throw a pillow at him.

That made us all decide to do the same thing, which we did.

But it was all a part of the surprise Santa

had planned for us. We were supposed to be awakened at midnight to listen to a special midnight broadcast from the radio station we'd visited. So we gathered out in the biggest room, where the canary had been but wasn't now, having been put in a covered cage in the kitchen.

Santa turned on the radio while we found places to sit on chairs and on each other's cots, and pretty soon the program was on.

And then all of a sudden somebody began to sing, and it was a voice *exactly* like Circus's voice, as clear as a bell, high and very resonant. I looked around quick, and there was Circus with a very funny expression on his already funny face. Then he scowled and acted bashful. Sure enough, it *was* his voice.

Yet it couldn't have been, because there he was, right in front of my eyes, looking sleepy and awake and bashful at the same time. And there was Little Jim too.

"It's *canned* music," Santa explained. "They made a tape when you were in the studio."

It surely was a beautiful song:

> My sins are forgiven, I know,
>   My sins are forgiven, I know.
>   Not through works of my own,
> But through Jesus alone,
>   My sins are forgiven, I know.

They'd made that recording, and Circus and Little Jim hadn't known it. If they *had* known, they'd probably have made a fizzle instead. All the way through the four stanzas of the solo, I kept thinking how very much I'd give if I had been Circus or Little Jim and could have had a sound recording made of something important that I could do.

But I couldn't do anything important—not sing or play the piano or any other musical instrument. I was just old freckle-faced, red-haired William Jasper Collins, who hadn't even learned how to control his temper.

And there were Little Jim and Circus, who'd already decided what they were going to be when they were grown up. One was going to be a gospel singer and the other a missionary, and I—then I remembered that I was going to be a doctor, a genuinely *Christian* doctor at that, and perform operations on people.

All the time I was thinking that—and maybe shouldn't have been, because it was selfish—the song kept going on: "My sins are forgiven, I know. My sins are forgiven, I know. My sins are forgiven, I know . . ."

Just then Little Jim slid over to me from the other end of the cot he and I were sitting on, and I looked down at his mouse-shaped face to see if he was proud of himself for playing so well, but he wasn't. I know, because he leaned over and whispered in my ear one of the nicest things I'd ever heard or ever thought of in my whole life.

"Do you know what I'm thinking about?" he squeaked.

Of course I didn't, so I asked him, "What?"

He waited till there was what is called an interlude between stanzas, which was piano music only, and then he said, "All those eighty-eight piano keys, from one end to the other, are going to be Little Jim's ladder, reaching up to heaven, and each one will be a gospel step for people to go up on."

After that I was ashamed of myself for wanting to be famous, so I tried to think of what I could do with a surgeon's knife that would help people's *souls*. There are a lot of people in the world—even right in Sugar Creek—who ought to have their *hearts* operated on.

Well, after the surprise, we all had to have a dish of homemade ice cream, which was already made and in the refrigerator waiting for us. Then we went to bed again and to sleep.

The next thing I knew it was morning, with another whole day ahead of us, and still another one after that, and with our most exciting adventure still unhappened, the one that was a bit like the dream I'd had at Sugar Creek that day when I was pouring raspberry juice into a boy's veins through a little tin funnel.

Never in my life will I forget what happened and why—and neither will Big Jim and Big Bob Till, because it happened to both of them.

10

On Saturday we did a lot of things and saw even more than we had already. The very first thing we did was to go to the Brookfield Zoo, where we looked especially for Little Jim's pet bear, which had had a white triangle on its chest, but we didn't find it.

You should have seen that zoo! Honest, there were more live things to look at and laugh at than you could see anywhere else in Chicago, especially the monkeys.

Once when we were standing in front of a bear's cage, watching three fuzzy baby bears eating their dinner in the way mammals do, for a minute I imagined I was back home listening to a million honeybees droning in the old linden tree that grows near the spring. If you've ever heard baby bears eat their dinner from their mothers, you know they sound like that. I could, for a minute, almost smell the perfume of the pretty creamy-yellow linden flowers I was thinking about. That is, until I smelled the bears' den.

The fuzzy little bears reminded Poetry of a poem that is good enough for me to write down for you. Here it is, which he quoted in his more-than-ever-squawky voice:

Fuzzy-wuzzy was a bear,
Fuzzy-wuzzy had no hair;
Fuzzy-wuzzy wasn't fuzzy,
Was he?

If you say that real fast, it sounds funny, and it is.

We went riding in two taxis, looking out the windows to see everything we could see. Hundreds of trucks and trailers were going both directions on one particular street, and all along the way were sad-looking, dirty-faced store buildings with people living in their upstairs. The saddest and dirtiest were the ones that were closed and for rent. The windows of our taxi were open, so with all the traffic it was just *roar, roar, roar* all the time, like the Sugar Creek threshing machine at harvesttime, when you're up close to it.

Then we went walking and saw different things. On the lawn of a big building called the Exchange Building was a sculptured stone bust of Abraham Lincoln, the sixteenth president of the United States.

Just as we walked past, Barry, who was behind us, said, "Boys, Abraham Lincoln was a farm boy. When he was your age, he hunted, fished, rode horseback, wrestled, and studied hard. He could shoot very straight with a rifle, and he made that a rule of his life—to be what is called a 'straight shooter,' which means he was always honest. In fact, he was called 'Honest Abe' by his friends."

I really can't take time to tell you all the things we saw, but it was worth the walk—and also worth the smell, although inside the entrance office of the meat packing plant we were going to see, the air was fresh and clean on account of the office being air-conditioned.

The meat packing place was interesting enough, but some of it was what Big Jim said was *gruesome*.

If you don't know what that means, you can look it up in a dictionary, which every boy ought to have anyway and ought to save his money and buy, even if he has to do without some candy and gum to buy it.

11

We ate dinner in a Swedish restaurant where you can eat all you want, if you want to. You can get up after you've had your first plateful and go back with a new, clean plate and eat all over again, which some of us did. I think the name of that kind of a dinner is called "smorgasbord." Poetry especially thought it was a good idea.

The Wrigley Building was next. While we were up in it, we looked down at a large parking lot, which looked very small from where we were. The cars away down there looked like toy automobiles.

"Look!" Dragonfly said, squeezing in between Poetry and me. "They look like a counterful of toy cars," which they did, and for once Dragonfly's eyes were right.

The afternoon flew by too fast, and also that night, and then Sunday morning came, when we all went to a boys' jail. And there we found out why the police had gone into the mission that night. They were actually after Bob Till, and they'd found him upstairs on the third floor, lying on one of the cots.

I guess I never saw Little Tom look so sad, because right on the front row, in a roomful of hundreds of boys who hadn't been trained up in the way they ought to go, sat Bob, looking down and looking very unhappy. His nose, I noticed for the first time, was hooked a little at the end just like his dad's nose is, and I thought that maybe his soul was just as crooked and that his dad had bent it for him.

But Little Tom had good stuff in him! He stood up right after Circus had sung his solo and told that big crowd of quiet-faced boys how he became a Christian, and when, and why he was glad for it. (You remember it had happened while we were all on our camping trip up north that summer.) He must have felt very topsy-turvy inside, because he kept swallowing.

His brother, sitting down there on the front row, had one fist on his right knee and the other on his left. Then he began to swallow too and to blow his nose, which is what a boy does when there are tears trying to get out of his eyes and some of them run down on the *in*side of his nose instead of on the *out*side. That's why nearly all people have to blow their noses when they cry.

It was when Big Jim was standing up giving the story of *his* conversion, which means when and how and why he became a Christian, that I realized how different he and Bob were. They were the same size and age, but that was about all.

Then Poetry, who was sitting beside me, called something to my attention. He leaned over and whispered while Big Jim was talking, "Look! Look at Bob's fists. They're all doubled up!"

They certainly were, and there were two fires in his eyes too. You could see that Bob hated Big Jim and that he wished he could spring right up out of his seat and knock the daylights out of him. You see, Big Jim was the only boy in the world who had ever licked Bob. The *only* one. Of course, Big Jim's being a great guy and with clean habits didn't help matters either.

Things began to happen fast after that. When the meeting was over, Barry and Mr. Farmer and the authorities at the jail talked a while, and there was some telephoning going on between Chicago and Sugar Creek. And the next thing we knew, Bob Till was free!

It happened that quick, although I found out afterward that there had been some telephoning during the night before also. Old Man Paddler had wanted Bob to be let out on parole because it wasn't good for a boy to be sent to jail for his first offense. They were going to parole him to Little Jim's parents, and he was going to work for them that fall. Mr. Simondson, our grocer, had decided not to bring charges, so Bob got out of jail.

The result was that when we left that morning, Bob was walking along with us. He even had on a new shirt, which Barry had bought for him.

He was giving Big Jim dirty looks, and I kept walking right along beside them on the way to the car, because I didn't trust Bob. The reason was that once I heard him swear at Big

Jim under his breath and say, "Think you're smart, don't you? Telling people you saw me breaking into that store."

"I did not!" Big Jim said, and his upper lip was trembling.

"You did too! And as soon as I get a chance, you'll find out Bob Till won't stand for anybody telling lies on him."

I sat beside Big Jim on the way to church, so I said, "You didn't tell any lies on Bob Till, did you?"

"Of course not," he said. "Nor any truths either. I didn't tell anybody anything, but he thinks I did because I saw him with my own eyes running out of Mr. Simondson's store that night."

Well, right after church it happened. We boys were all to ride to Santa's apartment on the El. He hadn't gone with us to church since he was preaching at his own church in another part of Chicago.

Zippety-sizzle, roarety-sizzle, bangety-sizzle, our elevated train threaded its way between the tall buildings. We sat side by side on each side of the car, looking at each other and out the windows, listening to the noises, and watching all the kinds of people who were riding with us.

Pretty soon we were in Santa's section of the city, which was called "suburban." The El came to a smooth stop, and the doors slid open. Out we went onto the platform. And there is where the fight bomb exploded.

I didn't get to hear who said what to whom,

but I heard scuffling on the platform behind me. I looked just in time to see Bob's very hard fist sweep around in a fierce circle and go smashing toward Big Jim's face.

At the same time Big Jim ducked, and Bob, who had swung with his whole body behind that blow, made a complete circle, his fist hitting nothing but some of Chicago's kind of dirty air.

It was such a vicious swing, and so hard, and Bob whirled so fast, that when Big Jim's jaw wasn't there to stop the fist, Bob lost his balance and fell backward over the edge of the top step. Down he went, his head crashing against the side of an old iron railing. My eyes could hardly follow him, he went so fast down that long flight of iron steps, *bumpety-bump*. He didn't even try to stop himself.

I guess I was the first one to see how he looked when he got to the bottom, since I was closest to the top of the stairway. I couldn't have moved if I'd had to. I felt just like a person does when he's looking over the edge of a *very* high embankment and is afraid. I was as weak as a sick kitten. Maybe I'd have tumbled down myself if my knees hadn't buckled under me and I went down *kerflop* on the top step.

The next thing right after that, Barry was flying down to where Bob was lying very still and white and—*red!* He was bleeding terribly from a gash in his head.

I got to my feet and scrambled down too, along with most of the Sugar Creek Gang and a lot of other people. But there weren't one-tenth as many people who had been on that El car as there might have been on a weekday, because, as I found out later, not even a fourth of the people in Chicago go to church on Sundays. There are hundreds of thousands of children who don't go at all, their parents making them go to school but not to church.

There at the bottom of the stairs, on a little platform where the stairway turned at a right angle before going down the rest of the way, was Bob, lying with his face on the end of a step, and he was pale and unconscious.

I was only halfway down those stairs when somebody went past me like a rocket, and it was Big Jim. By the time I got there, Big Jim and Barry were trying to stop the bleeding the way experienced Scouts know how to do. But they didn't have any equipment, and it wasn't easy.

Things happened pretty fast after that. They *had* to. You know, doctors nearly always advise a person *not* to move anybody who has been in a car wreck, especially if he's been crushed in the chest. There might be a broken rib that might puncture a hole in a lung like a boy puncturing a balloon, or else his smashed chest wall might press against his heart and kill him. They say in a case like that to keep the person lying very quiet until the doctor comes and let *him* decide what to do.

Barry, though, had been studying medicine. He saw right away there weren't any broken bones, unless maybe it would be a fractured skull, the bony framework of a person's head, where your mind lives. In fact, you live there yourself, and if your house gets smashed up, you have to move out.

I thought about that while we were on the way to the hospital where they were taking Bob. I thought, *What if Bob Till has to move out? Where will he go?* I knew he wasn't any dumb animal, and that he had a soul that would live forever somewhere, and that his dad would be pretty much to blame if he didn't go to heaven.

In fact, while they were carrying Bob's limp body—his new shirt all messed up and spattered with blood—to Santa's car, which was waiting for us at the El station, I wished every boy's parents would have Bible reading at their family table and would take their children to Sunday school and church. I even wished I was president of the United States, so I could help have a law passed that would *make* every boy in America go to church, whichever one he wanted to, at least once a week until he was twenty-one years old. After that, maybe he'd have sense enough to go himself and to obey God's laws.

I said that to Poetry, who was sitting beside me in the taxi.

"All right," he said, very seriously for him, "and I'll be vice president. We'll declare a national emergency and start the biggest war on the devil there ever was."

I'd never seen such a big hospital. There

were more sick people in that one hospital than there were *well* people in all Sugar Creek township! But it seemed to be a very wonderful place.

I don't know how I ever got to do what I did. Maybe it was because Barry knew I was going to be a doctor and arranged for me to watch what happened, which they don't generally let a boy do in a hospital.

They let me watch them give Bob Till a blood transfusion, which means taking blood out of somebody and giving it to somebody else. They *had* to give blood to Bob on account of his having lost so much, and maybe he couldn't have lived without it.

In fact, it looked for a while as if he might die that very afternoon.

12

The first thing they did with Bob after they got him into bed in the hospital, with nurses busy going everywhere in a white hurry, was to decide to give him a blood transfusion, and it would have to be done right away.

Pretty soon an official-looking nurse came in with a little tray that had some glass tubes on it. She looked around at all of us and then went straight to Bob's bed, rubbed something on his finger, and then pricked it with a needle.

"Wh-what's th-that for?" Dragonfly asked me, and I felt proud to think I knew what to tell him, because I'd already been studying and trying to learn all I could about medicine.

"That," I said with a grim face, "is to test his blood so as to find out what type it is, so she'll know what kind to give him. If you give him the wrong kind, the two won't mix right, and the blood cells will clump together and *kill* him."

I guess I said the last part too loud, for Tom turned as pale as his brother already was.

It took the nurse only a minute to do what she had to do, and then she was gone, and we were kept waiting.

"She's the laboratory technician," I said to the rest of the Sugar Creek Gang, trying to look very businesslike.

We learned they had in that hospital what are called "blood banks," which have blood all ready to give to people. As soon as they knew what kind you had to have, they opened one of the little banks and gave you some.

All the time, Bob was sighing and acting very weak and faint. I can't take time now to tell you all the different things the Sugar Creek Gang said to each other or what I thought while we waited, but before long I knew things weren't working out right.

The nurse I told you about, the "laboratory technician," found out that Bob's blood was what is called type B, and no more than seven out of one hundred people in the world have that. And the hospital didn't have any blood in its banks like that. They'd had to use it all that very morning for somebody else!

Things looked very bad for a while. Barry and Santa both had type A, so they couldn't use *their* blood. They already knew that, and they told the doctor so.

Big Jim was standing right beside me, with *his* fists doubled up, not ready to fight Bob Till but—I soon learned—to fight *for* him.

Suddenly Big Jim's doubled-up fists doubled up still tighter, and he walked over to the doctor, who had been out and had just come back in. They had been telephoning different people in the city who had type B and couldn't find anybody who could come to the hospital. One man lived on the other side of the city, and it would take an hour for him to get there.

So Big Jim set his jaw and walked toward that hospital bed and toward the doctor. I knew they wouldn't want any boy to be a blood giver, so I gasped. And again in my thoughts I was back in Sugar Creek, looking up toward the top of Bumblebee Hill, where Bob Till and his rough, swearing gang of boys were hollering at us and calling us cowards and Sunday school sissies. Then, with my mind's eyes, I saw Big Jim step out of the bushes where we'd been hiding and march right up the hill toward them.

"Fellows," he'd said that day, "it isn't a question of whether we're afraid to fight. There isn't a man among us that's got a drop of coward's blood in him!"

And now here we were in the hospital room with Bob maybe about to die, and Big Jim was going to prove that he still didn't have a drop of coward's blood in him and was going to offer to give his blood to save his enemy.

Big Jim, who had had a transfusion himself when he was little, happened to remember that *his* blood was type B.

That second I felt Little Jim's hand push its way into one of mine, and I knew that, if he could, he'd have told me something he was thinking about. I found out afterward it was a verse from the Bible, which says, "God demonstrates His own love toward us, in that while we were yet sinners, Christ died for us."

"How old are you?" the kind doctor asked.

"Almost fifteen," Big Jim said. I noticed he

was standing half on tiptoe to make himself look tall.

They had to telephone home to Big Jim's parents to explain it and to get their permission; and the technician had to check his blood with Bob's anyway to be sure it was what is called "compatible," which means they were friendly to each other and wouldn't fight. Well, they found out they wouldn't, and I couldn't help but remember Bumblebee Hill again.

They took Big Jim down the long hall and onto an elevator and up to the surgery room, and Barry and I were allowed to go along with him and the doctor and the technician and a nurse and two students who were just learning how to *be* nurses.

That was a funny-looking room. It had a great big chandelier above the operating table —which looked like my mom's ironing board but was longer and wider.

They laid Big Jim down just as if they were going to operate on him.

I couldn't see very well, because I had to peep through the open spaces between doctors and nurses who were standing around watching or helping. But I could see a little glass jar with a rubber bulb on top of it. There was a tube with a needle fastened to one end, and the other end was fastened to the glass jar.

Big Jim stretched out his arm for them to use. The next thing I knew they had a big needle stuck into one of his veins right in the crook of his arm, and then, with somebody working the rubber bulb, the glass jar began to show red in the bottom, and I knew Big Jim was giving his life's blood to save Bob Till.

Once he moved his head and looked over at me, and I looked at him, and I guess right that minute I never liked anybody better in all my life. I wished I could have dived in there and got hold of his other hand and squeezed it tight to let him know how I felt.

Higher and higher the blood line crept toward the middle of the glass jar, the brightest red I'd ever seen, brighter than the pretty roses that grow in Mom's garden. And then I looked at Big Jim's cheeks, and they weren't as rosy as they had been.

Maybe if I hadn't had Christian parents and a Sunday school teacher who believed the Bible, or if I hadn't happened to have Little Jim for a friend, I wouldn't have thought of what I did just then. But I thought for a minute of Somebody who had had *both* arms stretched out, and He was hanging high on a big, ugly wooden cross and was letting His very special blood flow out for all the sinners in the world. And now, whoever wants to can believe in Him and have everlasting life.

And for a bit my thoughts got mixed up a little. Instead of seeing Big Jim there, in my mind I saw Jesus, who didn't have a drop of coward's blood in Him but volunteered to die to save the whole world. And now anybody in the world who will trust in the blood of Jesus to wash away his sins will be saved forever and ever.

They gave Big Jim some kind of medicine right after that, and even though he was very weak for a while and a little pale, he didn't have much trouble getting over giving blood, because Big Jim was the kind of a boy who took good care of his body. He was proud of his strong body, and he let God be the boss of his health and his mind too.

I hated to leave him and go to watch them give the blood to Bob, but I thought I ought to so I could write it all down for you to read. (Some of these things I've had to ask Barry about, and some of them my dad, and that's how I happen to know the names for different things.) So pretty soon I was down in the hospital room with the rest of them.

In a jiffy they had Bob's arm ready. They put a needle in the vein at the crook of *his* elbow and hung up the glass jar on some kind of a stand that was a little bit like a cross, then let the blood run down through a long tube into Bob's arm. It went down very slowly, *dripping* in, somebody told me afterward.

The gang stood in a sort of football huddle, watching the whole thing. I kept looking at Little Tom's face to see how he felt about his brother.

Pretty soon, Bob's cheeks began to show a little pink, and then he looked better. He quit sighing, and in just a little while he was asleep, *and his life was saved.* Anyway, that's the story of the Sugar Creek Gang in Chicago. Nobody in the world ever had more interesting things to see, or had more fun, or learned more than we did. Of course, we still had to have that Sunday night meeting in the church, and the Labor Day meeting in Santa's church, but that's too much to put into this story.

We also still had ahead of us the airplane trip back home, and the next day after we got home we had to start back to school.

And that reminds me! We had a new teacher that year, and—as boys do sometimes when a new teacher comes—we had to find out the very first week whether she would stand for any monkey business or whether we had to behave ourselves *all* the time.

We tried different methods, but none of them really worked until the day Poetry tried to do what the girl in a poem did once. He let one of his dad's pet lambs follow him to school.

This lamb had to have a rope tied around its neck before it would follow Poetry, though. And before he got it to school, it fell into a mud puddle, and its fleece wasn't as white as snow when it got there. Neither was the schoolhouse floor after the lamb had walked around the room a while. All that was before the teacher came that morning!

I guess I'll rest a while before I tell you about what happened when she did.